The
DRAGON
KNIGHT

Anonka

authorHOUSE®

AuthorHouse™ LLC
1663 Liberty Drive
Bloomington, IN 47403
www.authorhouse.com
Phone: 1-800-839-8640

Published by AuthorHouse   09/04/2014

ISBN: 978-1-4969-0836-0 (sc)
ISBN: 978-1-4969-0835-3 (e)

Chapter One
The Starting

It all started in a time of chivalry, in a time and place when man and beast could communicate. It's a time lost to the distant past. The record unfolds to reveal the innocent, to reveal the trusting, to reveal the brave, and yes, to reveal the magnificent. This story is very much needed to help mankind weave a peaceful life from the dim pieces of his past. We are the crafters of our lives, the builders and designers of the human self. Therefore, we can rebuild our lives from the lumber of our past. Here, within these crinkled pages, you may find enough cognitive tools to evaluate your past, your present, and the makings of a beautiful future. You see, only you can do it.

Our story began eons ago, many calendars before this present day. It was not so far in the past; people passed the story from generation to generation. King Kohler and Queen Quess ruled from their wooden thrones. They lived in a large castle of green marble, colored stone, and specially spilt rock. The king and queen used much of their wealth to spread among the people. They lived in cooperation with the people who lived on their land. Those who were healthy and worked more received more.

Those people who were healthy but didn't want to work received less, and those who were ill received no help. The king and queen forgot no child. The very young had the opportunity to learn skills so that they could grow up to take pride in a trade. The kingdom developed an efficient water filtration system for dwellings and land irrigation. Farmers developed an eco-friendly growing season. People befriended animals and made use of them as friends, protectors, and show, but they did not eat them. Food consisted of fruit, nuts, vegetables, and some flowers and herbs. A large brown bird of plenty and a certain killer fish were on the food list too. Twice a year, the king and queen planned a special get-together for everyone in the kingdom. A large screen was set up all around the grounds, so people could congregate and see the king and queen.

Now, King Kohler had heard the tales of the court many years before him. There was a story about a dark, deadly dragon, a dragon among dragons, the biggest of them all and the ruler of them all. The king heard that very dragon needed to be destroyed. On the other hand, the king also heard through the whispers of his kind people that the dragonkind was a peaceful one. He would shame those that came to destroy him without spilling any of their blood. It is known by many people that dragons are not killers.

The dragonkind would build a shield to make them invisible to humankind. They were only visible when the shield was down. Dragonkind could throw flames a mile in front of them from the methane gas in their stomachs; they used this gas to clean the caves, cook killer fish, and to compete in dragon tournaments. Dragons chose not to kill humankind or others in their realm. They were known to make threats, but they would not kill. The threats were enough to frighten away those who would harm them.

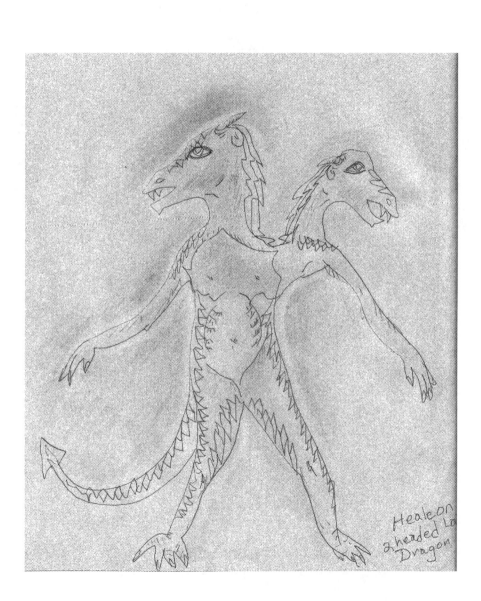

Healeon
2 headed Lo
Dragon

Chapter One A
A Plan Put into Force

The king and queen were plotting to take care of the dragonkind once and for all. My question is this: what were the king and queen's hearts? We will find out as the story unfolds. Born to the king and queen was a princess, an only child called Celia. Of course, she was the fairest in all the land. Beautiful Celia was held dear to the people of the kingdom.

But to return to the dragons: the king and queen posted a notice in the courtyard. They were certain that their plan would work. If a truehearted man could bring in a mighty dragon unharmed, that man would, whether or not he was a knight, gain the hand of their daughter in marriage. What a strange action for a father to take—giving away his beloved daughter in exchange for a dragon. Do you think this king knew something that he wasn't sharing? Perhaps he did not believe he would have to honor his promise.

Celia and an agent named Theodore Payper were in love, though it was unclear to her whether or not her parents knew this. Many knights wanted Celia as their wife, but their fear of the dragonkind prevented them from pursuing her.

Many knights tried and failed to capture the dragonkind. The knights believed it was impossible to bring a dragon in alive; no one had ever successfully accomplished it. The village worried and gossiped about which of its men was brave enough to catch a live dragon.

How many knights went out to seek the dragonkind, I do not know. This, I do know: Theodore Payper was not a knight, and yet he packed his bag to go in search of the dragonkind. He had no idea how he would perform such a huge task; all Theodore knew was how much he loved Celia. The king handed Theodore a long brown canvas and burlap bag. The Queen took Theodore to the side and told him, "Just remember, knightless Theodore, nothing is rarely what it appears to be." Theodore took the piece of bark Celia gave him with a message on it which read: "Failure to plan is a sure plan for failure."

She also gave him a handkerchief with her name on it. The Queen gave Theodore a little black book of memories. In his long brown bag, Theodore packed a little vile of magic potion—he only needed a little, because the potion was so strong. He also packed a sliver of silver foil—he only needed a sliver, because silver foil is so reflective. Theodore also packed a dirty box of town dirt, because the dirt from your birthplace reveals a lot about where you came from. He packed a bottle of heavy bubbling bubbles; bubbles are useful, remember that. He carefully packed the lace hankie with a kiss and the name of his sweetheart on it. Theodore packed his tiny black book, which held his memories, and a vented satchel of nine fat fireflies, plus many other good things. Wait a minute, we can't forget his shoes. He packed two extra pairs of walking shoes. Theodore gave kisses, said his good-byes and off he went to the West. The West was where new discoveries were made; the North was where knowledge was learned; the East was the place of memories; while the South was a dry, hot place that had no other use except as a hideaway.

Did he choose the right direction? We shall see. His best friends shouted to him, "Go west, young man." Off Theodore went, with people pushing him out of the large stone gate, the gate that led into the fortress. People blocked the gate so Theodore couldn't return if he wanted to, which he didn't.

Chapter Two
Regaining Confidence

Theodore could feel his temples pounding like a drum inside his head. His heart was racing so fast, it was as if he was passing himself by. His strides were so wide he couldn't believe they were his feet taking him away. Actually it was deep glorious love that moved him onward. When he thought of Celia, confidence filled Theodore as he moved swiftly along an unknown course. He had no idea what he would face or if he would survive.

Theodore traveled a day before he realized he'd forgotten to bring food or water. I guess Theodore wasn't as prepared as he should have been, but perhaps it was all part of his plan. Just then his stomach started to growl like a big, ugly monster. His lips were sticking to his teeth from thirst, but on he went and on he went and on he went. Our forgetful Theodore passed out on the ground with a thump. He slowly got to his feet but stumbled. Without pause, he weaved himself to a strange berry bush. Reaching his hand out to pick a berry, he then placed it in his mouth. To Theodore's surprise, the berry was watery, delicious, and filling. So, perhaps he had planned to survive from food on the road. Sometimes we have plans that our conscious mind knows nothing about.

Theodore lay back down on the ground and rested his head on an old, knobby tree trunk and drifted off to a much needed deep sleep. Theodore awoke; he was refreshed, alert, and ready to continue his unknown journey. He thought he was three days away, but he had a lot of road to travel. Theodore got up to his feet with a jolt and ran to the strange berry bush to gather berries to replenish him on his travels, but to his shock, the berries were all dried up. Without giving it another thought, he piled about eight handfuls of the shriveled berries into the large pocket of his bamboo vest.

"Yum, yum," he said out loud. He pressed on and regained his confidence by thinking of his love for Celia. The woods grew denser;

the darkness grew blacker; his steps grew shorter; and he started to grow weary. He thought he had been traveling for four or five days and could no longer take another step. Theodore couldn't even move at all—it was like the woods had closed in around him and were about to swallow him alive. He reached into his bag and pulled out the satchel of nine big, fat fireflies; he opened the satchel and set them free. Lo and behold, the blackness became brighter; the path opened; and his steps grew longer. Theodore was on his way again, with the fireflies illuminating the path.

Theodore moved into what he thought to be the sixth day. He was taking out the brown, dried-up berries to satisfy his hunger and thirst and again regained his confidence; he began to sing. His song went like this:

> I will travel the road, not feeling the weight of my load; it will all get lighter and the sun will be brighter. What I think is what I know, as strong as the winds may blow, marching through it all, even if I stumble and fall, getting back to my feet never admitting defeat. I'll weather the storm feeling warm, even in the snow. I will bring back a dragon, not a dove, and will win the hand of my precious love. It's all in the thoughts; they will take you where you want to go. Your mind can't be bought, but it can put you in the know. If you complain and wail, you set yourself up to fail; if you laugh and grin, you set yourself up to win.

A small yellow bird sat upon his head and chirped along to his song.

To Theodore's amazement, he was soon flocked by these odd-looking birds—thousands of them gathered to his side. Never has Theodore seen birds such as these. They had long necks, fluffy green and orange feathers, and they were smaller than a humming bird. As he walked, he kept his head up, looking at the birds. Puzzled by them, he didn't watch his step and fell flat on his face. The birds dove down upon him; hundreds and hundreds of birds pecked wildly at him.

He said to them, "Bubble me birds; take a bottle of bubbles for each kid. Have them blow bubbles in the air. Run around saying 'no trouble me bubbles. Me bubbles bring no trouble.'" He quickly reached into his bag and pulled out a bottle of bubbles and blew them into the air. Theodore had no idea what effect the bubbles would have. The tiny birds flew up into the air chirping happily after the bubbles; they had lost interest in him. "Think"! he said to himself. "Never give up thinking; never give up. Your thoughts give you ideas; your ideas give you hope; hope leads to discovery; discovery brings action; and action is what can save you." Theodore walked and walked and walked some more.

He stopped to pick up some stones, stones in all different colors. They were beautiful, beautiful stones. He pulled some bright thread from the trees and wove the colored stones together as he walked. He made the stones into wristlets, he thought they may come in handy some day, and it helped to keep him busy as he walked. Theodore put the wristlets in his long, brown bag. He dragged the bag behind him; because it was much easier to carry that way. (Is that what you would have done)?

Chapter Three
The Heat Experience

Theodore thought he had walked seven or eight days. He took a break and leaned against a large, green rock. He wanted to evaluate all the strange and wonderful things that had happened to him. He pondered whether or not he was dreaming or awake. Theodore had never set foot in these woods before; he has never traveled outside the protective confines of the castle walls. The castle is surrounded by nine hundred thousand acres of choice farming land. It is surrounded by a stone wall. People live, work, and play within the safe confines of the castle's walls. They think the walls help to maintain a good, healthy lifestyle. Is that what you think? Or would you say that people must do the work to ensure their own health?

Theodore pinched himself. Ouch! He must have been awake, so he moved onward. As he plunged into the unknown, he felt both excited and afraid—excited about the new adventures he expected to encounter and afraid he might not have the ability to overcome the fears.

Then he thought, "I have already faced the greatest fear that every castle dweller fears, going out beyond the protected barricade of the castle. There's no knight to defend me, no armor to shield me, and no guide to keep me on a certain route." Then he knew, just as he always did, that if he was to accomplish his goal, he must do so by himself. Excitement overrode his doubt and fear, but he also knew that his fear might crop up again. If it did, he would take care of it. Theodore thought he had been walking for twenty days or so when he stopped in his tracks. "What in the world is this?" he wondered as he looked at an area devoid of grass and trees.

"This area appears to be hard and dry like a desert with stones," Theodore said aloud as he wondered if he should go forward or backward. He couldn't go back—going back wasn't really an option, because of his love for Celia. Instead, he plunged forward across the strange, black desert land. He releases a scream that would rip your ears off: "Wow! It's not a desert—it's quick sand!" Under he sinks as he whispers a bubbly good-bye to his sweet Celia, "Goop-bye Cebla." Blackness overcame him. Wouldn't you say good-bye to a loved one?

Theodore woke up lying flat on his back, staring up at short, reddish natives with long, skinny necks. They were jumping and yelling as they circled around him, "Uggie, ougie, ongie." The rest pointed to a group of natives preparing a narrow trail about forty feet long. Two of them picked him up by the arms and dragged him over to a hut. They took his shoes off as they tossed him inside. Theodore was in the hut for what he estimated to be two hours. A female opened the flap and placed a water jug inside the hut and disappeared for another two hours. Three more ladies stepped inside the hut carrying clothes and face paint. They gave him coarse bread and grayish water. The women cleaned him up and dressed him. One woman painted his face with red, yellow, and black paint. Theodore ate the dry, hard bread and drank the grayish water. He immediately passed. When he awoke, he believed it was the twenty-third day, but he couldn't be sure. Do you know? Two of the natives dragged him out of the hut to a narrow trail of red hot coals. A native slapped the bottom of his bare feet and pointed to the trail. Theodore yelled, "No!" and shook his head.

All at once the natives screamed wildly, "Uggie, ougie, ongie." They danced around him in a fever while two of the natives dragged him over to a stump where a huge elephant was tied. That was it for Theodore—he let out a loud scream: "Yes!" as he shook his head yes. They lifted him up to his feet and brushed him off carefully as they led him to another hut. This time it was filled with clear, blue water, rich goodies, plus unbelievably beautiful women without long necks.

Theodore ate and drank to his heart's content, but he wondered what he would have to face at the pit.

The women were the most beautiful women he had ever seen; they didn't look anything like the natives, but it didn't matter, because his mind was on Celia. Theodore stayed in the hut another two hours as they tattooed one of his arms—the entire arm. Theodore sat clenching his teeth, looking at the women and waiting to meet his fate at the pit. Two of the natives walked in and stood Theodore on his feet. They bound his arms behind his back, blindfolded him, and shoved him out of the hut. After several paces, they stopped. Someone folded up both pant legs, gave him a firm pat on the shoulder, and a strong push.

Theodore took a deep breath as he plunged forward; heat permeated his nostrils, and dripped heavily from his forehead and down onto the smoldering red coals. He could smell the hair burning on his arms; he was sure his lips were bubbling, and his eyes felt like they were going to melt out of his head. How could he stand anymore? All the while, he could only think of Celia. *Oh, Celia, how I love you,* he thought to himself.

Theodore felt two strong arms grab him by the shoulders. They spun him around and removed his blindfold off. Lo and behold, he had made it to the end of the long, hot trail. He was alive and had sustained no burns, no burns at all. The natives appeared to be happy: they were dancing, singing, and throwing flowers in the air. Two of the most beautiful maidens brought him his belongings, and poof—the maidens disappeared with a puff of smoke.

Theodore stood there for a while—shocked at what just happened and feeling pretty damn proud of himself. The natives came up to him one by one, saying, "Congratulations, you're free to go. You are a true heart. With our help, you have made the right choice." *What? They could speak my language the entire time?* he thought. He didn't question it. He just waved good-bye as they dragged him safely through the quicksand on a sled. Theodore felt good and strong, knowing he could stand whatever came along or could he?

If you want to find out., read on. Are you a true heart like Theodore? Soon you will find out if you are.

Recipes

Red-hot Dottie; Take a glass of V Eight Juice. Put some very hot sauce in it. Stir with a celery stick. As you drink, say, "I can make it. I can make it. I can make it. See, you made it. You're a true heart.

Onie cakes: Get some small strawberry cakes at a store. Put a scoop of ice cream inside the hole. Drip some caramel topping over the ice cream. Pour melted hot fudge over that. Serve and enjoy.

The Bone Dragon

Chapter Four
I Want to Go Home

By now, Theodore thought he had been walking for twenty-five days. He walked on and on into through the twenty-seventh day. He kept track of the days every night fall. He thought he knew how long he'd been traveling, but he had no idea then how wrong he was. Theodore made his way deep into a wooded area, and bang!

Just like that, he was out of the woods. *What kind of place is this?* he thought to himself, looking around at his new surroundings. There were piles of rocks, and lots of stone, a little grass, and hardly any trees. Theodore heard something up ahead that sounded like water rushing over rocks. He ran forward and saw the largest body of water he had ever seen. The white sands and rocks glittered in the sun.

Theodore thought, *This sure is mystical. Maybe I'm here. Maybe I made it; maybe the dragonkind live here.* Theodore stripped down to his onesies (one-piece underwear) and prepared to take a well-earned dip in the cool water. In he went, face-first. After rolling around in the beautiful water, he crawled onto the beach spitting and coughing. *My goodness,* he thought. *I've swallowed a mouthful of water.*

Theodore fell onto his back and lay on the warm sand, his arms and legs spread out, and yelled out loud: "What am I doing here?" He screamed even louder: "What in the heck am I here for? I don't want to be here in this dumb place. I have no reason to be here. I want to go home! I want to go home! I don't even know where home is! I don't know who in the world I am." Theodore scrambled to his feet. For what felt like days and days, he wandered around aimlessly. He realized he was slowly dying of hunger and thirst. Accepting his fate, he looked around to find a soft place to die. He saw his long, strange brown bag, It looked so soft, *A place to die,* he thought. *First I must look inside the strange bag.*

Theodore found this little black book. As he opened the black book of memories, he started to remember a little. Was that his mother? Was that his father? Were those his sister and brother? It hurt to remember, so he slammed the little black book of memories shut.

Theodore lay his head on the soft bag and closed his eyes to welcome death. But then he wondered about what else was in the book. Theodore opened up his little, black book of memories again, and he remembered his home; he thought of his friends; he thought of the king and queen; and then he remembered Celia. *Oh, my dear sweet Celia* he thought.

He remembered everything, even his name. "My name is Theodore Payper," he said.

Theodore looked further into the bag and found his bamboo vest and the dried berries. He ate a few and felt refreshed. He realized the water had caused him to lose his memory. Little did he know that if he had taken another drink, the water would have restored his memory. Of course, we know, and he didn't know. You know, because I told you so.

Recipe:

King And Queen Smiles: Cut an apple in fours. Spread peanut butter on one piece. Put another apple piece on top of it. Place tiny marshmallows like teeth. It looks like a smile.

Chapter Five
Now What?

Theodore had put in quite a few miles when he saw these little bugs flying around him. He started to swat at them when he realized they were fairykind. *Wow,* he thought to himself. *I've heard of fairies, but I've never seen one. They look and dress like little tiny people, but they have transparent wings and can fly real good.* Now he could see hundreds of them; he was trying to understand what they were saying; they were all talking at the same time in tiny voices. Theodore said, "Stop! Only one at a time can speak. I can't understand what you're trying to tell me."

One fairy said, "You must keep your course."

Another one said, "Or you'll wind up back where you came from."

Another one said, "Set a while."

Still another said, "We can help you."

Another one said. "Yes, we can."

Theodore heard a puffing sound. When he looked around, he saw a fairy his own size. She put her hand on his shoulder and said, "Sit" as she push him down a little. Puff, puff, puff, puff: they were all his size and back to talking all at once.

"Silence!" A red-haired fairy said. "Each one can speak in due time. This good man needs some assistance."

"He needs a shiny silver compass," said another fairy.

"A golden timepiece," said another fairy.

"And a fairy horn," said different fairy.

A green-haired fairy gave Theodore a large sponge and told him, "You are going to need this; you are really going to need this." As each fairy spoke to him, another fairy gave him the things he might need during the rest of his journey. Eventually, he had stowed all the items neatly in his brown canvas bag.

Theodore gave each little fairy a colorful stone wristlet that they wore around their necks, and when they enlarged themselves, they wore them around their wrists. They sung, "Thank you, thank you, oh yes, yes, thank you." Their voices were so soft and lilting. Away Theodore went thanking them all, one by one, as each Fairy kissed him on the cheek, leaving glitter behind. It took quite a while for each fairy to kiss him on the cheek.

Fairy Dessert: Take a whole tub of strawberry whipped cream. Mix with a cup of powdered sugar. Spread all over a strawberry angel food cake. Make sure to fill the hole. Pile the top with strawberries. Serve with pink lemonade. Clink the glasses and say; "To the wee little fairies."

Fairy Kisses: Take some very fine glitter, and apply it to your upper lip. As you kiss someone on the cheek, say, "You've been kissed by a fairy."

Chapter Five
AB

Theodore thought for a moment, *Who else will I meet? Little greenkind from the moon?"* and he laughed to himself. Theodore turned around abruptly, because he thought he'd heard someone jumping behind him. Sure enough, someone was jumping. A little greenkind jumped around him and said, "Don't call me little; I'm all of four foot tall chalked on a wall, plus I can't fall with my neon jumping boots that I'm jumping with. Would you like to jump too?"

"No, thank you, Mr. Greenman," Theodore said. "I'm okay just the way I am, but thank you."

The little greenkind pulled out a pouch and said, "Here's your own pair of neon jumping boots. You will need them where you're going," and, poof—he was gone. Theodore thought, *How would he know where I'm going?* Theodore put the neon jumping boots in his brown bag and away he went. But first Theodore tried on the boots and began to jump when the green man reappeared.

The greenkind said, "Let me help you learn to use your neon jumping boots. Kick your heels, boy. Kick them with each foot—that gets them started real good. Now jump and keep jumping> No matter what you jump off of, you will always bounce, no matter how high; it is safe to jump. Your neon jumping boots will never come off, even if someone tries to take them. The only one who will be able to remove them is you, when you chose to take them off. They will always stay together; they won't be parted. If you go away and forget your jumping boots and you find you need them, all you have to do is call them. Just say, 'My neon jumping boots are made for jumping; come to me.' Say it a couple times, and they will be in your hands—happy and ready to go to work." He was gone just as fast as he got here.

Green man jumping cookies: Put green frosting over a cookie. Each person can use a cookie to jump over another cookie. Say, "I'm all of four foot tall, chalked on a wall."

Chapter Six
A Gypsy and Her Horse

After a few miles on the road, Theodore met a ladykind in a caravan. She had a mass of red hair, a mass of pearls, a mass of jewels, and a mass of big, wide full skirts—in short, she was amassed with everything. The cart had these wooden wheels that went around and around, but what was marvelous was that one of the horsekind was pulling the caravan. Theodore had heard of the horsekind, but he had never seen a real, live horse.

The Gypsy lady said, "Climb aboard, young feller. Give your feet a rest while you tire out your bottom." She was holding a strap that led to the horsekind, as she asked Theodore, "You know anything about horses?"

"My goodness, no," said Theodore. "Do you know what a horse is"? asked Theodore.

The Gypsy woman answered, "They are more agreeable than a jackass. You see, boy, I had this jackass, and was he ever stubborn. I never knew where I would wind up with him leading me. When I said left, he went right; when I said right, he went left. Oh my, I found myself in the strangest places all the time. He was one adventure after another, but anyway . . . that darn jackass up and died on me. I cried for weeks and weeks.

"So, one day I saw this field of horsekind, and I sat on a rock for days waiting for one to come to me. I was whispering to it; do you know what that is? At least, I think I was whispering to it. So, I got him, and I tied myself to his back until he calmed down, Whoa! What a ride. That darn horse had spitfire in him. But I can't get him to go where I want him to go either, and I have to hope I get to at the place I want to be."

"He must have some jackass in him," Theodore said. "Maybe if you had a double strap, then you could pull one strap one way and pull the other strap the other way till you got him to go the way you wanted. So, the Gypsy tried Theodore's suggestion, and it worked. She was as happy as a lark, or as happy as a Gypsy could be.

The horsekind said, "Heeee! I've been trying to tell her that for days, heeee! Double it up, I said, double it up, but oh no!"

The Gypsy yelled in frustration at the horse: "Shut up! I told you! You can't talk!"

The horse continued, "When she sat on that rock, I tried to tell her, pick me, and I'll come to you. But oh no, she just sat on that darn rock for days before choosing."

Just then the Gypsy hit the horse on the rump with the strap and said. "Shut up I told you, you don't know how to talk. Or I'll do some cutting where you don't want cut."

"Whoa!" said the horse. "You're the lady; I'll shut my big mouth . . . for now, anyway."

Theodore told the lady, "I can hear the horsekind talking, so he *can* talk. Maybe you should listen to him."

She said, "Yes, yes, I think I'll do that." Then she asked Theodore if he would care to stay a while, explaining, "We never get your humankind very often—well, not the kind that won't steal from me. Say," she said, looking up, "will you steal from me when you get the chance?"

"No, no," soothed Theodore, "I've had so many goodkind give me so many good things of such good use, that I could never ever think of taking a thing from any kind, it would stop them from giving me things.

"Yes, yes, that is how it works. I'm glad you know that some people always want to take what other people have instead of waiting to be given gifts," the Gypsy said. The horsekind and the two humankind talked and talked for hours. When evening broke and the Gypsy was sound asleep in the caravan, the horsekind told Theodore to climb on his back for a good night's nap, so he did. But Theodore and the horsekind talked away half of the night. Theodore asked the horse what his name was. The horsekind was so happy that Theodore had asked him his name that he shared the strange story of how he got his name.

"My first master filled my mouth with my own blood because I didn't have any lips; he made lips for me, because he felt sorry for me, because I couldn't say 'few,'" and the horse rippled his lips as he blew out.

"So, my young mankind, take a guess what my master named me," said the horsekind with a slanted smile.

"I can't guess," said Theodore, 'but please tell me."

The horse stomped his hoof a couple of times in the grass as he said, "He named me Fill-Lip, that's what he named me. What do you think of that?"

"Fillip," Theodore repeated, "That's a good name; I like it. Well, Fillip," Theodore said, "I think it's high time we went to sleep. Thank you so much for the nice conversation."

"It's my pleasure," Fillip said, and then Theodore heard this lips flipping, and when he looked Fillip was fast or maybe slow asleep— so Theodore went to sleep too.

The next morning Theodore and Fillip opened their eyes and started talking to each other. "Good morning, my new friend," said Fillip.

"Good morning, my new friend," said Theodore back to him. The horse went out to the pasture to eat some green grass and clover and Theodore went over to the Gypsy's campfire and ate her Gypsy fry bread with sugared berries and hot chicory drink. After they had a hearty breakfast, the Gypsy turned to Theodore and said, "I have potions, lotions, and all kinds of notions—what would be your treat?"

Theodore said, "I wish I had something to ward off this heat."

The Gypsy quickly said, "I have some of my home dome hair tonic to block the rays of the sun; here it is." Theodore tried it, and it worked. It felt as if the sun had gone down. Fillip, the Gypsy, and Theodore traveled together for days and nights—laughing, talking, eating, and then laughing, talking, and eating again.

When the Gypsy got into a wooded area, Theodore asked to get out. As he said his good-byes to his two new friends, he said, "I hope we will meet again."

Fillip said, "Yeah."

Theodore told Fillip and the Gypsy, "Someday I want to treat you both to a meal at the castle where I live."

Gypsy said, laughing, "Oh yea! I bet! You sure look like a guy that lives in a castle."

"Oh yes; oh yes," said Fillip. "I know; I know as sure as I live and speak, Theodore. You live in a castle, and you are a prince, a prince of a prince. Yah, yah."

The Gypsy slapped Fillip on the rump and said, "Shut up, you dumb animal, or you'll get a—"

Fillip stopped her in the middle of her sentence, as he snorted, "I am not a dumb animal. I can talk; I can think; and I know a truthful man when I see one, and Theodore is a truthful man. Never use that strap on me or threaten me again, or you won't get to go visit my good friend, the prince."

Theodore asked the Gypsy not to strap Fillip again, "because it is not a nice thing to do; please tell him you are sorry."

The Gypsy told Fillip, "I am so sorry for my meanness; you are my friend, my only friend, and we can talk together. I will never lay a strap on you again. I thought I was stupid because a horse could talk better than I could."

Fillip and Theodore said good-bye to each other. The Gypsy said, "Merry meet and merry part, till we merrily meet again. That is a Gypsy good-bye, you should try it some time."

Theodore said to himself, *Oh my goodness, how I love those two. I know I will see them again, oh yes. I will make sure I see them again.*

Gypsy fry bread: You'll need flour, baking powder, and water. Put grease in a warm pan. Spread out small, flattened balls of the dough and fry until brown on one side, then turn. It is good to cover them and make sure the heat is low. Mash berries with sugar. Cook them a little, spread on the bread, and enjoy.

Chicory drink: Now I will tell you how to get this hot chicory drink. At the side of the road you will surely see this petty blue flower— some say it's purple. Dig it up, and brew the root. It will taste like a sort of coffee. If you like it, drink it and enjoy it, because it is so very good for you.

Chapter Six DD
Lords of the Underworld.

Soon Theodore walked into a clearing when he saw a sign that read, "Come down and meet the lords of the underworld." He'd heard of the underworld, but he didn't know what it was. Some people have said it was bad, but he thought *I will find out for myself.* Theodore slid down a tunnel until he reached the bottom. It was dark and was musty. He met a little brown bunny with a light on the end of his nose. The bunny's light flashed in the face of a mole, the mole said, rather grumpily, "Get that light out of my face. You're blinding me; ain't I blind enough?"

Theodore asked them if they knew the way to the underworld. He explained that he wanted to meet the lords of the underworld. A couple of chipmunks came sliding up behind him and said, "Hey buddy, where do you think you are? This is the underworld, and we're its lords."

The mole remarked, "Where did you think you were?"

Theodore said, "I see. I'm glad to meet you guys. Just what does an underworld lord do?"

"We dig, dig, dig, and give advice to the lords of the upperworld, that's what," they answered.

"Is there some advice you can give me?" asked Theodore. "I could use all the advice I can get."

"Learn to dig; all must learn to dig; all must learn to dig," they all said at once. The bunnykind handed him a pair of gloves with finger nails on the ends. Once Theodore got above ground, he thought, *Whew! That was strange, but they were very nice, and they were not bad in any single way.* Theodore put his new digging gloves in his brown bag, and away he went, off to his next adventure.

Theodore

Chapter Seven
The Neon Jumping Boots

Theodore got to the edge of an ocean and his timepiece read "go across if," but how could he cross it? It was a deep, blue ocean. He took out the shrunken sponge the fairykind had given him and laid it front of him. The sponge soaked up a narrow path for him, and across he went, dry as could be. At the end of the path, Theodore kicked the sponge, and the path closed up again. *Great*, Theodore thought.

Theodore felt something big pick him up by the arms. When he looked up, he saw a great, giant eaglekind. The eaglekind put him in her nest, then flew away. Three huge eagle eggs were in the nest with him. He knew when the eggs hatched that they would eat him alive, or they would eat him up dead. Theodore started to kick at the eggs to break them, but it was too late; they were hatching. He thought about the neon jumping boots, so he hurried to put then on and jumped out of the nest to safety. Theodore said out loud, "Thank you, Mr. Greenman."

Then he heard a voice say, "Oh, that's quite all right. Didn't I tell you that you'd need them?"

Theodore replied, "Oh, yes you did tell me, and I thank you. You saved my life."

Theodore thought he'd do a little traveling at night, which was fine until he passed a pack of gray-and-white wolfkind; then he started to shake. But they didn't bother him in the least; they were busy howling at the moon. They just blinked their eyes at him as the leader spoke, "We are not a threat to mankind, but mankind can be a threat to us. You are one of mankind, so we will run to safety. We only kill what is sick and dying, and you look very healthy." They went to a cave where Theodore could see only their bright eyes blinking out at him, so he knew he was safe, and the wolves were safe too, because

Theodore would never hurt them. Maybe some of mankind would, but not Theodore.

Theodore came across a family of raccoonkind, who said, "Out of our way, please. We are heading for a can of trash. Sorry, there's not enough to share with anyone. The mother raccoon said, "I must first think to feed my little ones." Now Raccoons are unusual mammals; they nurse their young using their own milk, and they are also carnivores (meat eaters) Raccoons have five toes on each paws and can use them like hands, and they will eat almost anything. Some say they wash their food, but it's not true. Raccoons will go through the motion of washing even if they don't have water; it's a motion they used to make when they fished in the wild.

Theodore smiled when he saw a mother opossumkind. She said, "Hurry, hurry, gotta go. Hurry, hurry, gotta go, gotta go before the sun breaks."

All the babies on her back squealed, "Me too, me too, gotta go, gotta go, bye, bye," and away they all went. The night was so nice; the moon was so full; and when Theodore looked, he saw a night owlkind. The old owl said in a squeaky voice, "Whoooo . . . are youuuu? Whaaaat time is it?"

Theodore looked at his timepiece, and it told the owlkind,. "His name is Theodore, and it is five in the morning, and this is a sleep warning." So Theodore lay down to take a nap. When Theodore awoke, his timepiece said, "It is high noon; gone is the moon, and it's nearing June. Jump to your feet, eat some sweet, then hit the street." Theodore looked around, but he didn't see a street, nor did he know what a street was, so off he went. Theodore walked for what he thought was five hours. When he asked his timepiece how long he'd been walking, his timepiece replied, "Snakes alive, it's quarter after five. We must strive, ask these people why do they strut with a bare butt?"

Theodore looked around and did see people with their butts hanging out. Theodore thought, *There's no back to their pants; how strange.*" A big yellow-and-red sign spoke aloud, "You are in the land of Honalee;

stand and take a pee on an old oak tree," so Theodore did just that. One of the humankind with holey pants said, "Why do you think we are strange when it is you who's strange?"

Theodore said, "well, why do you all strut with a bare butt?"

One of them replied, "We strut with bare butts so we can strum with our bums and fart to get a good start. We couldn't even dance if we had a back to our pants."

Another one looked up at Theodore and yelped like a dogkind as he said, "Take off the back of your pants and dance as you eat this bean fruit; it will help you go toot, toot." Theodore noticed that every time they farted, they moved four feet forward, but the smell they left behind was like sweet bubblegum.

Theodore did as they instructed him to do. He ate the bean fruit, danced, and farted all night long. It had been such great fun, but now he was done. They gave him some bean fruit for the trip so that when he grew tired of walking, he could eat some bean fruit and move forward. Theodore thought, *I have met such nice creatures. I hope I see them all again. Oh yes, I know I will.* One of the bare butt men said, "We come from inside the moon and we visit in the month of June. Come back now and then so we can play you a tune."

Wolf Crackers: Pile a cracker with peanut butter. Put some chunks of jerky on top of the peanut butter. Howl at the moon. Fun, yeah? You can eat it too.

Trash Can Treats: Take a piece of white bread. Top with apple butter spread. Pile on everything you can think of. Raccoons love it. You will too.

Bean Fruit: Cook butter beans, and chill them. Mix with lots of fruit. Yum, yum. Eat to your fart's content—it will be music to the ears.

Chapter Eight
One Last Wish

Theodore waved good-bye to the nice bare butt people and went on his way. After all, he couldn't stay any longer, because he had a job to do. Theodore had to find the mighty dragon and bring him back alive so he could marry his beloved Celia. Our brave, knightless Theodore saw a group of people ahead of him. He pushed his way to the left, and he pushed his way to the right before he saw what was ahead. He saw several people throwing stones at a poor, little lady. He stepped in front of her and yelled, "Stop." Theodore said, "Let the person without shame cast the first stone." They all started throwing again. Theodore yelled, "Stop! Please stop throwing stones."

The people were shocked that he wanted to save her; even the poor little lady was amazed at his concern. "What is it to you whether she lives or dies," said one of the stone-throwers.

"Yes," said another. "She has to die this way or a harder way."

The ladykind was crying as she spoke, "Please, go your way, and let me die in peace, and maybe I will be forgiven."

"What!" Theodore shouted. "What makes you people think you have a right to kill her? Please tell me."

A fair-skinned, yellow-haired man walked up to Theodore and said, softly "Don't you see her red hair, green eyes, and devil's marks?"

A very, very large man yelled, "Strap them on the ten-foot pole and take them both to our sacred grounds; they will both be dealt with later." So Theodore and the old woman were taken to a clearing where hundreds and hundreds of humankind were standing around clapping and cheering.

Theodore could see the big, giant building in the background. It had millions of dollars' worth of strange, giant things. He thought to himself, *They all can't be heartless; someone has to have a heart.* But to his dismay, the crowd happily took part in the ritual. Some were yelling, "Glory to me in the tree."

One tiny, little old ladykind said softly, "The tree says, suffer a boy-less not to live." Then she yelled, "Burn, boy-less, burn."

Others screamed, "Kill the soiled!"

The very, very large man yelled, "They will die in great pain as our land demands; come, let us rub the soil for their wicked souls." They were preparing two stakes as Theodore noticed a cage of large, fat-necked, hungry birds trying to get out. He heard the people cheering for the birds to pick away at Theodore and the lady. "Dear me, oh my, oh, may their pain sustain us; we do this in your weeds, oh sweet land," they repeated. Theodore and the ladykind were laid out on the ground while the men poured honey all over them.

Smart, witty Theodore made one last attempt by saying, "Thank you, humankind, for granting us one last wish."

He repeated it several times until someone said, "It may be fun to see what their last wish could be, as if it would help them! Ha!"

Theodore said, "The land orders you to bring me my brown bag,"

Someone responded, "Do you think us stupid enough to believe that the land would talk to the likes of you?" But they brought him his brown bag. Then, Theodore took out the bean fruit, and Theodore and the ladykind both ate some. Soon, Theodore and the poor lady sprang forward, as Theodore bellowed, "The land moves us in happy ways; it's trees for you to behold." Off they went in leaps and bounds, four feet at a time. The crowd stood there in shock.

Theodore repeated several times, "The land says no more pain; the land says no more pain; the land says no more pain."

The crowd yelled back, "No more pain; no more pain; no more pain; the land commands no more pain."

When Theodore and the poor ladykind got to safety, the ladykind started to cry, "You have saved me only to drown for all time."

Theodore made a face and said, "What could you have done to make you think you should die in such pain?"

She explained, "I went against the land. I only had girls; I didn't have any boys . . . I'm shameful." She added, "You, sir, are water-bound too, because you tried to save a wretch like me. I'm going back to face my punishment."

Theodore reached his hand out to lean against a tree. He took a deep breath and proceeded to speak. "All manmade dirty lies are better not believed; life is better without self-made lies; life is safer keeping self-made lies out of it. Even the old stories tell us it started out to control humankind."

Theodore slid down the tree trunk and sat at the base; he watched the poor lady walk away. He kept talking as she moved out of sight. "Some of humankind invented the self-made lies along with the idea that the lands were invented to serve them. That's why they inserted into the wooden trunk what the head-human wanted. The promise of obedience was a heaven; the punishment of noncompliance was a hell. It was easy for the contriver, because when people start to believe lies, they become addicted to them. Why believe something just because someone said you had to believe or die a bitter death? Why hold on to addictions created by self-serving people? Why, oh why? Why not check it out?" Theodore put his face in his hands and cried; all his talking was just a waste. She had gone to her death. Theodore couldn't walk the opposite way knowing she was going to die; he had to try his best to save her. Because, that was who he wanted to be—a good-hearted man.

The poor lady reached the crowd, and again they were clapping, and again they huddled around a woman. She just stood there waiting, waiting for them to take her, to take her to her death. Theodore ran up to her; he had to put his hands on his knees, he was so out of breath. When he saw the crowd huddled around another woman, Theodore thought. *Oh no! Another ladykind to try to save.* He jumped in front of her and yelled, "Stop, in the name of compassion," but this time they were cheering the birth of a newborn baby girl, a new baby born to the newly loving town. They wanted to care for each other without hatred, dominance, and lies. The very, very large man said in a soft voice, "Come friend, feast with us at our bonfire. You have showed us a new way to live, a good way to live, the best way to live—with love instead of superstitions and blind beliefs." The poor ladykind, whose real name was Lady, told her people all the good things Theodore had told her. Yes, she had heard him, but it took a while to sink in.

The people cried in shame and then in happiness. The very, very big man said, "We were bound by chains of self-made fear that held us captive; now we are free, free to think, free to love, and free to be happy." Theodore stood watching the fire burn away the artifacts of the blind belief—large, worthless things, twisted black trees, and hateful paintings. *Could this be true? Theodore* thought. *I intended to help her, and I've helped a whole village—how wonderful.* Theodore waved good-bye as they threw kisses his way.

"Come again," they said. "You're always welcome; all are welcome now." *How wonderful. Love takes over where hate once ruled,* Theodore thought to himself.

Blame Me Chowder: Start with green cooked lima beans, yellow corn, and purple cabbage. Make sure everything's cooked and blend together. As you eat say, "I'm bad. I'm bad. I'm bad. You're bad too."

Baby Girl Pudding: Take white pudding and add pink food coloring. Little girls love it. Dress it up with sprinkles.

Chapter Nine
The Women Lead

Theodore moved on to the next town feeling confident again and happy to be alive. A tall, thin man met him at the gate to the town and extended a welcome. Theodore thought, *How strange—everyone is tall and slim and looks alike even down to their hair color, and they're all men. All the buildings are green, blue, and yellow. All the clothes are pink, orange, and purple.* After spending more time in the town, Theodore noticed there were no babies or children.

The humankind didn't seem to laugh. They were friendly, but they didn't talk a lot. Theodore also noticed that there were no fruit trees in the whole town. Theodore thought, *I need to talk to these nice humankind; I have to help them if I can and if they want me to. I'd sure like to see them laugh.* Theodore asked a man standing on a corner leaning against a short street light, "Do you have a mayor? I'd like to talk to him if I could."

"I don't know," the man said. "Can you? Can you talk? Mayor, Mayor?" The townsmen walked around saying, "Where is the mayor? Can anyone find the mayor?"

Theodore said, "I'd like a meeting with the mayor and the town board, whoever they may be." Just then a large black limo drove up with a lady in a black suit at the wheel.

She opened the door and said, "Get in." Theodore got in and sat in the back of the limo, and waited to be told to speak. *This is strange,* he thought. *This is very strange, but I guess nothing is strange after all I've seen and done.* The ladykind in black drove about five miles outside of town. It was a virtual paradise with hundreds of fruit trees, fields of flowers, and lots of children and babies; they were all laughing and playing. He could see buildings in white and black—it all looked so happy. The ladykind in the black suit told Theodore to step inside the courthouse. as she pulled out a chair for him, he sat down and started to talk. "Do you have a mayor, or a town council? I'd like to talk to someone."

The ladykind put her finger over Theodore's lips and said, "Be still; you'll have your chance to talk." Other ladies in black came in and sat around the table. They too were tall and slim, and their hair was black.

One seat was empty at the head of the table. Within minutes, a very, very tall ladykind walked in and sat in the empty seat. She slammed the gavel down and said in a firm voice, "Who brings us to this meeting? Speak up! Who calls for this meeting?"

Theodore stood up and, in a soft voice, said, "Thank you ladykind for giving me a chance to speak at your council meeting. May I address the mayor?" and he sat down.

The tallest ladykind at the head of the table spoke without standing, "The mayor was exiled to a prison island for raping children, and he can never return. I am the mayor now: tell me what you want."

Theodore tried to choose his words wisely as he spoke: "My esteemed ladykind, I don't have a problem. I am not from here and am passing through, but I wondered why the men are separated from the ladies and children. I realize it is none of my concern, but I'd like to be of service and help, if I can."

The tallest ladykind said, "The meeting is called to order, and the floor is open for discussion." Everyone said, "Aye," and one after another spoke their piece. This is a summary of what they said.

People who commit any criminal acts, such as cheating on spousekind, beating wifekind or childkind, are given three chances to reform. After that, they are taken out of town until they seek help and improvement. They can return, but only if they have recovered. If not, they are sent back.

People with religion are permitted only in a church of the same kind, or in their own home. Anyone who harasses others to join their religion or brings religion outside of church will be locked up for a period of five Sundays—mankind or womankind. If they keep doing it, they will stay on the prison island. Some of the brave mankind have volunteered to work with other mankind to help guide them to be more sensitive to emotions and feelings.

Good ladykind are the leaders, the shapers, and the voice in the town. Mankind will soon work beside them but never over them. If our arrangement works out for the best, in a year or two, we will move our towns together and live in harmony and peace. One of the ladykind spoke up, "We get together once a day with our loved ones. We speak about how things are done—both mankind and ladykind."

Another ladykind addressed the meeting: "Towns were disinfected everywhere and ladykind have become leaders. We have strong rules that we enforce, and our communities are safer and happier."

Theodore said, "It looks like you're doing good, and you're so right. Thank you for your kindness and openness." He spent the night on the side where the mankind were, and they were good, and it was so good. He thought the night away, *Women are sensitive, for the vast majority mankind is the problem, not ladykind. Many ladykind are devoted to family and friends. It is such a good idea to have women become leaders and healers. It is so right, so very right. If people just thought about it, I know they would agree.*

Black And White Sauce: Make country gravy. Separate the gravy, and put black food coloring in half of it. Pour both colors over biscuits or potatoes. Say, "May we all work together."

Chapter Ten
Is It the Dragon's Lair?

When Theodore awoke the next day, he got dressed, put on a new pair of walking shoes from his bag, and went into the wild blue yonder. Theodore was skipping, whistling, and singing. He felt fortunate to be alive and back on track. The people in the town had helped him to think about his life and feel better about himself. Theodore wasn't trying to keep track of the days anymore; he'd lost them when he'd lost his memory. He walked and walked and then walked some more. He felt good and knew in his heart that things would be all right. Theodore knew he must have been walking for days, because his timepiece told him, "You have been walking for days and days, so put your head where it lays." He lay down on a soft spot of lawn, ate some berries, and went to sleep. Theodore awoke the next day refreshed and ready to go; he used his map piece to choose his direction: north, south, east, or west. Theodore walked briskly swinging his arms and singing, "I've got a blue jay on my shoulder." Pretty soon there was a blue jay on his shoulder.

He was so happy and filled with confidence, with the blue bird chirping away as he sung. Theodore came to an area that was so thick with brush, pickers, and twisted vines that he had a tough time getting in; he kept trying to push his way though. After what seemed like hours, his timepiece told him, "It has been hours, don't get the sours." Soon, he was in a clearing. He stood at the base of a mountain with a waterfall behind him. Theodore saw thousands of giant flowers and lots of beautiful hummingbirds. It was such a wonderful place; the flowers must have been at least ten feet tall or more.

Theodore stood there admiring the scene. He heard a strange sound to his side; he turned and saw a cave as big as a mountain; in fact, it *was* a mountain. He watched carefully, standing very still, and didn't move a muscle. He wondered what would come next. Theodore saw the side of the mountain cracking, splitting, and breaking up. The cracks formed a name: Gorbash. Theodore stood there in front of the mountain for what must have been hours; he didn't know what to do. His timepiece told him, "You're in the grove, so make a move."

Well, he thought. *I must do something.* He took out the golden trumpet the wee fairies had given him and blew it three times. Then he thought, *Could Gorbash be the name of a dragon?* Theodore's mind told him to close his eyes and rush into the side of the mountain. So he did just that. When he opened his eyes, he was inside a cave, and the opening closed behind him. Theodore never even thought about how he'd gotten through solid rock. Instead he looked around the cave and marveled at its beauty and splendor.

Stalagmites in rich shades of purple, green, and pink reached up from the floor at the sides of the cave. Crystals as large as men richly adorned the cave; many hung from the ceiling. Theodore was shaken back to his senses when he heard a low rumble from the back of the cave. Fear grabbed him by the nape of the neck; his hair stood straight up like sharp little needles. Never had he ever been so scared. He felt like he'd swallowed his Adam's apple.

He cried like never before, out of fear. Yet, to his own surprise he yelled aloud, "Are you the great dragon?"

Just as fast as Theodore spoke the answer came back. A very deep, craggy voice yelled, "What manner of effete man wants to know? Answer expeditiously you puerile of puerile."

Theodore replied, just as quickly, "It's me, Theodore, and don't call me moron. I think moron is what puerile means," he answered, shocked at his own daring.

The voice grew louder. It shook Theodore so terribly that he wet his pants. The voice rippled back, "I'll call you whatever I wish to call you, you tiny obtuse thing called man."

Surprising himself, Theodore yelled back, "Stop! I come to your home to visit you, and you treat me like dirt." He threw the dirty box of dirt from his brown bag in the dragon's direction. Theodore started crying softly to himself, "I'm really going to be in trouble now."

The mighty dragon stepped into the clearing from the dark shadows of the cave. Our dragon is twenty feet tall, with a wingspan of twenty feet. The scales down his back were a deep green, but they're light green on his underside. The scales around his eyes were slate gray. His eyes were a deep amber color that seemed to light up. This dragon stood straight up and made slow, long strides from right hip to left hip. He had very white teeth, and his mouth and tongue were bright red, as were the bottoms of his feet and hands.

The first thing that Theodore noticed was that the dragon was covered in dirt—the dirt inside those little boxes had multiplied. "Theodore," said the dragonkind, and it echoed: "Theodore! Theodore, Theodore." The dragon laughed loudly, "I know where you came from, little man. You have traveled from the land of Chardonnay—the dirt tells me your whereabouts, but it doesn't tell me the quest you are on. Since you are a man, it must be an abominable quest, one that would bring harm to dragonkind," remarked the dragon. "Tell me, brave, moronic Theodore: just what *is* your purpose here? Your courage should be congratulated—it's clear that you're terrified," said the dragon as he slowly moved in closer.

Theodore stepped back a few steps, quite a few steps as he took out the silver sliver of foil from his bag and flashed it in the dragon's face. Rollicking laughter filled the cave, as the dragon told Theodore he had the foil backward. Theodore turned the foil around, and immediately the dragon said, "This tells me about you and your so—called sweetheart, but it doesn't tell me about the hearts of the new king and queen."

Theodore snapped back, "I can't vouch for the king and queen, but can't you try to trust them?"

"Trust them?" snarled the dragon. "To you, trust is just a simple word; for me it's certain *death*."

"I trust them," said Theodore. "I trust them, because I have no choice. I'm in love with their daughter, and I have to bring you back alive in order to marry her."

Gorbash snapped back, "Well I'm not in love with their daughter, and I do not trust mankind, but I will give *you* the benefit of the doubt. I hope the doubt won't outweigh the benefit."

Theodore started to relax a little, and he thanked the dragon: "Thank you, Mr. Dragon, for your trust."

"Not trust: I do not trust your kind," yelled the dragon. "Don't confuse trust with doubt; I'm only giving you the benefit of the doubt. That doesn't mean I trust you." Then Gorbash snarled as he said, "If I gave you what your kind gave us dragons, your head would be rolling down a mountain at the speed of a rock, with your broken body tumbling not far behind it."

Gorbash quieted down a little to say, "Now you shallow excuse for life, climb up behind my ear. There's a pocket and a handle for you to hold onto, and I'll take you to the pond of knowing, by the wall. You can call me Gorbash, but don't think for one moment that I'm being friendly." Gorbash growled aggressively and bared his teeth. Theodore crouched low and shook with fear.

male Vampire Rednor Blood Dragon

Chapter Eleven
The Pond of Knowing

Theodore climbed aboard and they were there in moments, without even leaving the cave. Theodore looked deep down into the pond. It was clear green and filled with water lilies and tall sticks, but that was all. Theodore sat down on a crystal chair and wept like a baby. "You lied to me. Do you take me for a fool?" Theodore asked bitterly.

"You pitiful excuse for a man—of course I take you for a fool, because you are a fool," snapped Gorbash. "I'll call you a fool and a moron until you stop acting like one." Gorbash told him to ask the pond for what he wanted to see. Theodore felt silly talking to a pond of water, so he backed away. "Idiot, after all the strange and stranger things that have happened to you, you choose to feel silly *now?*" asked Gorbash.

That was it. Theodore called out to the water, "I want to see what my Celia is doing." The image showed her trying on a wedding dress. Theodore fell backward on the ground, pounding the rocks and yelling. "I want to die; I want to die; my love is getting married; let me die." Theodore screamed at Gorbash, "Squash me like a bug; drown me like a rat, and then swat me like a fly." Theodore paused and said, "Wait a minute; I'll let her know I love her, and I'll be there before she knows it." Theodore got up, ran over to the pond and yelled, "Oh, mighty pond, let my love know that I love her and that I will be there soon."

Gorbash stopped him from continuing and told him, "Wait! Little moron, it doesn't work that way; you can only get it one way." Gorbash went on to tell him, "You've been gone over a year; maybe they think you're dead, but then again, maybe they're stupid enough to be waiting for you." Gorbash looked over the water and asked, "Are Theodore's puny people still waiting for him? And does the king's daughter love him?" Just then an image appeared of the king and queen and Celia; they were talking to each other. "Be patient, our daughter," they told

Celia. "You have your wedding gown, and Theodore will return; the court jester told us so." Celia said, "Oh Mommy and Daddy; I know he's alive, I can feel his love."

"The wedding gown was for *your* wedding, you Lilliputian pile of tripe, and you wanted to die. Why I let you into my lair, I'll never know," snarled Gorbash. "But as long as you're here, you embryonic person, I'll summon you into my living quarters." He took Theodore beyond the entrance of the cave. His so-called home was twenty-five miles wide and twenty-seven miles long; he had an open dry skylight the size of it all. There was a waterfall to the left, with a pond and beach as well. It had a garden to the right with fruits, vegetables, and flowers, and the garden had its own sprinkler system. Would you believe he even had a fairyland within these acres? The trees were the most beautiful Theodore had ever seen.

Little brightly colored huts were scattered throughout the area, and wee little people in green were walking in and out of the huts. They were elves. But what Theodore saw next amazed him even more. He had never seen such things. The tallest was fifty feet tall, and the shortest was two feet high. It had cups, buckets, and turtle shells. He saw something called a wheel that went round and round and a propeller that spun so fast you couldn't see it anymore. Theodore saw a round thing that other things bounced off from, a drum that clubs pounded on, and a thing called a slide that other things slid down. There were large rings that other things flew through and more and more. Everything was somehow connected. When it was done, it started up again.

Also, there was this thing that went hundreds and hundreds of feet up in the air and down again fast; it would safely hold a dragon or a wee man. It was like going up and down a hill, only much faster. Gorbash called it a roller coaster, and Theodore loved it. The whole place would maintain itself.

Theodore stayed with Gorbash, talking to the elves and fairies, and loving every minute of it. Gorbash softly said (as soft as a dragon could talk), "Theodore, you effete being, I will go with you to Chardonnay. Do you feel better now?"

Theodore danced all around the dragon's lair and cried, but this time he cried with happiness. "Thank you Gorbash," declared Theodore. "You are by far the best dragon I have ever met."

"Yes, you addle-pate," said Gorbash, "but 1m the only dragon you've ever met. We shall see if you still feel the same when you meet the other dragons." Just then Gorbash let out a sound that made Theodore hold his ears. Gorbash was known as the navigator; he could find his way around anywhere, anytime, and back again. Gorbash was the eldest of the dragons; he had lived for hundreds and hundreds of years. Many kings and queens had come and gone during his life. Gorbash was sought by the kingdom a hundred times over. The knights of the palace tried to bring him down, they'd wanted to take his head to the king, but they had failed every time.

But some of the dragons were killed, and the dragonkind were slowly declining. Now that there was a new king and queen, Gorbash wondered what they might have up their royal sleeves. The pond of knowing could not tell him; it grew cloudy whenever he asked. Gorbash had great sorrow from the past; it caused him to dislike and doubt mankind, for mankind hunted and killed dragons. Dragonkind could not live in peace, because the knights of the kingdom hunted them.

Chapter Twelve
Marta and Yagoo

About five hundred years ago, Gorbash had had a mate. She was called Marta and was as green as Gorbash, but her green was a variegated green. Her eyes were jade green, and her feet and hands were small and blue. She had a short stride as her tail moved with a swing from side to side. Marta was only eight feet high and had a wingspan of seven feet. Gorbash was so happy with her and delighted; she was due to birth a new dragon any day now. At this time, dragons give birth the way humans did—with their eggs inside. There had been a time when both dragons and humans laid eggs, but both had evolved for the protection of their young.

Gorbash had warned Marta not to go outside the cave without the protective field, but, in a hurry, she did just that. The king's men killed her and tried to take her head away when Gorbash saw them. He spit out a flame that could have turn them to ashes, but it only sent them away. It was too late for his mate Marta; killing the men would not have brought her back.

Gorbash noticed his son trying to get out of his mother's body, so, as quickly as he could, Gorbash opened her up and took him out. Gorbash's little offspring was bluish green with shades of light gray. He was all of two feet high with a wingspan of two feet, and the bottoms of his feet and hands were pink. The little dragon walked with a shuffle and blew out streaks of yellow and red. He was born with fuzzy hair on his knees and shoulders.

Gorbash knew he had no way to feed him; dragon pups needed their mother's milk. They could survive a few months without it before their scales would fade and fall. The mighty dragonkind was with his offspring for only three months. He learned to love him, bonded with him while frantically trying to find food his son could eat. He named him Yagoo, which meant "life," because he wanted Yagoo to live so very much. One day when Gorbash was holding him and tickling him under the wing, some of Yagoo's scales started to fall off.

Yagoo watched his scales as they fell to the ground, picking them up and turning them around in his hand. Yagoo sadly asked, "Father, am I to fade? Am I to die? Please tell me, Father." Gorbash couldn't speak; he just hung his head and wept.

Yagoo then knew he was dying, so he said, "Father, I do not wish to leave you. I know you will be so lonely without me; please keep my scales in a covered bag. It will help you. I will look for Mother in the cave of death. I will tell her of our bond. Thank you, Father for being the greatness you are; my time with you has been so precious." Yagoo died, softly saying, "Thank you, thank you, thank you." Yagoo's bright scales faded, and they all fell off as he slowly turned to ash.

Gorbash planted the remains of his mate and offspring, along with some of his own blood. He put them under a tiny flower seed. He lay down beside them and wept for ten years. When Gorbash got up, he saw the flowers had grown to ten feet and were every color of the rainbow. One could easily see why dragons had a difficult time trusting mankind. Gorbash could have easily killed Theodore, but killing was not in him. All he could do to serve his broken heart was to call him demeaning names. Our great dragon wanted to help everyone, even at his own risk, which was why he was willing to accompany Theodore.

Theodore asked Gorbash, "Why are we going to take other dragons? How can we get in touch with them? Are all dragons in tune to each other"?

"You infinitesimal gnat," Gorbash said. "We will take other dragons, because I say so. Now, be still while I ready for the trip. By the way, it will not take us as long to travel to the castle as it took you to travel here, because I am not a moron." Theodore watched Gorbash retire to the back of the giant cave. As he listened, he could hear Gorbash transmitting. He was sending some kind of message. Lots of bright lights went on and off along and made strange, clicking sounds.

When Gorbash came to the front of the cave, his scales were a deeper and darker green and had a shine that surprised Theodore. "Put your brown bag behind my left ear, Numskull. Place your bag in the pouch," ordered Gorbash. "We will only come back here for the wee ones; we will all live, thanks to the king and queen; or we will all die, no thanks to the king and queen," declared Gorbash. "Either way, we will not come back here."

So, up they went, up through the top of the cave, and out through a crystal skylight. There were many crystal skylights throughout the cave, anyone of them could have opened into an exit. Only the dragon of the cave, however, could have opened them.

male half cat half
Dragon

Chapter Twelve
Half Dragon! Half Fish?

When Gorbash and Theodore got outside, Gorbash said, "Be very quiet. Something is splashing in the water; stay here on the shore. I must check it out." When Gorbash got closer to the area, he saw what it was. It was a dragon, but not just any dragon. It had gills and large fins but it was definitely a dragon. As Gorbash got closer, the strange dragon approached. Then it dove underwater, resurfaced, and dove again.

When Gorbash got to where it was, it surfaced right in front of him. Gorbash wasn't shocked; he knew of this fish-like dragon, but he had never met him. The knights said the creature didn't exist; the dragons thought that he did, but they had never met him, either. Now Gorbash was face-to-face with a legend—what would he do? Gorbash started to talk to the gilled dragon, and the dragon answered each and every question. The gilled dragon spoke as if he were underwater.

The gilled dragon was a loner; he kept to himself for fear of the human knights, fear he may be slaughtered. He told Gorbash he has never met another dragon since he'd lost his mate. He met three knights that sailed the deep blue sea; they killed his mate and offspring then tried to kill him. This underwater dragon lived in an underwater cave, which had one opening. Gorbash asked the new dragon his name.

"I am called Seagon, and I'm aware you are the great Gorbash, the wisest and strongest of all dragons," answered Seagon. "I am not without my wiles, a useful art that has kept me alive for all this time," commented Seagon.

Gorbash rolled back with a question, "To what do we owe the unexpected pleasure of your acquaintance, Sir Seagon?"

Seagon answered in a rather deep voice, "The pleasure is all mine, new friend. I received news of the treaty that may come to pass, and, if at all possible, I would like to be part of that treaty."

Gorbash told him, "Come with me to the shore, Seagon, and meet the human that has braved the journey in the hope of making the treaty a dream come true for us all.

As Seagon approached the shore, Theodore could see he was almost twenty feet tall with a wingspan of nineteen feet. His wings wrapped around himself while he swims. Seagon was a dazzling blue with swirls of white, which made it difficult to see him while swimming. Theodore spotted a blow hole on top of his head like a whale's, which showed that he sometimes needed air underwater. He had gills on each side of his neck, which helped him stay underwater for long periods of time. He had five, long webbed fingers on his feet and hands that enabled him to swim long distances.

Now this dragon did not spit fire; instead he spit great amounts of water. This proved helpful for him. Seagon saw Theodore and became unnerved. He turned back to the water. Gorbash said, "Stop, Seagon. This is not a knight; he is a good-hearted human and will do you no harm." Immediately, Seagon spat out a profusion of water that flooded the shore. Theodore coughed and coughed and almost drowned. Gorbash yelled, "Seagon, stop. You have hurt an innocent being; come back and apologize.

Seagon slowly returned. When he saw that Theodore truly was innocent, he got on his knees and begged forgiveness. Theodore told Seagon that he would never hurt anyone. Seagon replied, "Many have said that, and many have lied. That is how I lost the ones in my care; that is why I am alone. Now tell me truthfully, one called Theodore, have you ever wanted to hurt or harm another being?"

Theodore looked at Gorbash and said, "Yes I have, but I am sorry now."

Seagon said with a frown, "I thought so; you have a little darkness to you, and sorry doesn't cut it."

Gorbash quickly interrupted, "Seagon, while what you say may be true, I must interject. We've all experienced great losses. We are here now to gain something. When one points a finger at another, he must be ready to have a finger pointed at him. Are you ready, Seagon, for finger-pointing? All this time you have been alone, but you didn't have to be alone. There are many trustworthy beings here. You chose to swim in self-pity; we all must learn to act for the future instead of reacting from the past. This one called Theodore has taught me about my mistakes by seeing his, and likewise I'm sure. In every class of life, there is only a small percentage of those who wish to do us harm."

"Gorbash," said Seagon," if what you say is true, then I have lost more than I'd ever thought, but then again, if what you say is true, I risk my life for a good reason." Seagon added, "I must add for the sake of knowledge, I am not a fish of any kind, maybe a dragon of another kind, but in no way am I a fish. Although I may have some of the abilities of a fish, I remain a dragon. Do I make myself clear?"

Gorbash and Theodore said together, "You made yourself clear as water." As Theodore climbed up behind Gorbash's ear, Theodore asked Gorbash, "Gorbash why did you call Seagon *Sir?*"

"Because he is royalty, little gnat, because he is a king himself," replied Gorbash.

Chapter Thirteen
How Ugly Are the Ugliest

Seagon flew ahead to watch for danger, because he could coast with ease during flight. After a day and night in flight, Gorbash landed to replenish with food and water, and Theodore ate more of the wrinkled berries. Seagon wasn't far in front of them. He flew swiftly, from side to side, watching like a giant blue hawk with his mirror like eyes.

When Gorbash took to the air once more, with Theodore in the pocket behind Gorbash's left ear, a sticky net covered the mighty dragon. Gorbash told Theodore to remain quiet and stay where he was. He then explained what had captured them. "These things," Gorbash said, "had been thrown out of their own time and space because of their diabolical doings." Gorbash went on to say, "They have a type of glass syringe inside their mouths to drain out all the life fluid of their victims. They go behind the head at the nape of the neck. Once the needle is in, the artery is severed, and the brain is disrupted, killing the victim. Then they proceed to suck the fluid from the body. They've never tried to take a dragon as a victim; they must be very hungry."

Theodore peeked out at the creatures and felt sick; they were gray and brown with four arms that wiggled uselessly at their sides. Their arms were lined with suckers, however, which allowed them to climb up the sticky net. They had four legs that could hardly hold them up; even with that handicap, they stood about six feet tall. He saw they had sagging fat and their bodies reeked of boils and scabs full of green puss. Their creepy eyes sunk into their heads and yellow fluid dripped down their faces. They squirted snot straight out of their noses.

Theodore could see lots of lumpy brown waste trailing the ground behind them, and the largest creature (or so it seemed to Theodore), had big lumps around his neck for the others to suck on. Only the lead creature got to suck from the victim, while the others sucked the fluid from the leader's neck ring. The smell was enough to make you puke. "Theodore, take the gavel out," said the mighty dragon. Just at that moment Theodore got out the gavel the ladies had given him, when the horrible creature approached Gorbash with its mouth open. Theodore smashed the creature's glass syringe a dozen times or more, and the ugly thing fell to the ground screaming and crying in pain.

It said, "You dirty rotten grub; you destroyed my sucking needle, I don't have any more left, because of you we will surely all die, unless you save us." The thing went on to say. "Whatever happens to one happens to us all." Theodore demanded that the creature set Gorbash and him free. Theodore and Gorbash were stuck in the net and couldn't get out. Seagon flew in and splashed something on the net that melted it, freeing them.

Gorbash let Theodore down and told him, "I know what you are about to do; it is an abominable thing, and it saddens me, as they are already dying because I told you to take out the gavel.

Theodore told the ugly creature, "Open wide for chunky the magic potion." Theodore poured all the bean fruit and all the bubbles down his throat. Within seconds, they were thrashing around and wreathing in horror.

The ugly thing said in pain, "You vile maggot; you lied. You said you were going to save us."

Theodore quickly replied, "Oh no; I only said that I would free you. When you die, you will be free, you ugly crappers." Theodore told Gorbash, "Let's get out of here before the crap hits the sky," and he laughed. Theodore got back into his safe place behind Gorbash's ear. They were a reasonable distance away when the explosion threw ugly chunks a mile away. The combination of so much bean fruit and so many bubbles together caused a backup of gas that couldn't escape until it exploded.

Gorbash hung his head in sadness and told Theodore, "I cannot laugh with joy when another life is dying."

Theodore replied, "Ha ha. Well, I sure can, when it's something as foul as those uglies."

Gorbash said in a soft voice, "Yes, I know you can. How well I know you can. After all, you are part of mankind, and they take pleasure in killing. But I must thank you for saving my life."

Seagon said, "See what I meant, Gorbash? This one wants death, but all I wanted to do was free you both. I will fly ahead now, but remember, Gorbash, telling someone how to kill is as bad as killing them yourself" And away he flew. Gorbash hung his head; he knew Seagon was right.

Theodore asked Gorbash, "What is that colorful building over there by the big orange trees?"

Gorbash landed and told Theodore, "That is their building; let's take a look at it." The building was stained glass from top to bottom and contained some of the most beautiful designs Theodore had ever seen. Theodore asked, "What is that wonderful colored stuff that lets light in?"

Gorbash told Theodore, "That is like the glass syringe. glass is made from hot sand. When there is a lightning storm, it leaves patches of hard sand. These ugly creatures come from the future; their people must have put the building here for them." Gorbash turned to Theodore and said, "Take a look at these uglies; for they are your future. They're mankind's future: hate, greed, and overeating. What a way of life: greed, food, and hate."

"Eat not what roams the land, but what grows from the land. Choose clean water and clear thinking not hate, and overeating," said Gorbash. "Theodore, you must learn to teach your kind to be better."

"I'm full of questions, Gorbash," said Theodore. "Why is it you know so much? Does Seagon know as much as you do?"

"Yes, yes; he does. Okay, Theodore, I will tell you," Gorbash said quietly. "But you must never tell anyone what I'm about to tell you." And he laughed softly

Gorbash went on to say, "If no one is born, this whole world of people will die in less than one hundred-and-twenty years—all will be dead. Everyone alive now will be gone. But you know that, don't you? All will be gone except us dragonkind. We live for hundreds and hundreds of years, and then some. Your learning will stop when you die, but this is not so for dragons. We live a long, long time. What we learn will pass through to the minds of our young, but only truth will pass through.

"Humankind can learn from books, but they must be careful what they read, for it can enslave them, for they do not always learn truth."

"But how else do you learn so much?" asked Theodore.

"Thought is alive; if one can think it, one can do it. We do not wear down our bodies, and our age is genetically controlled. Also, we transmit our thoughts and experiences, and others transmit theirs to us. That is one way we learn so much, but some things are better left unknown, added Gorbash as he turned his face away from Theodore. "Someday we will tell your humankind about nature' life path. It is a wondrous topic, worth talking about. It happens if you believe it or not, for it brings the truth to light."

Just then Gorbash noticed one of the uglies was alive. Theodore ran to stab him when Gorbash yelled, "Stop, Theodore! Why are you in such a hurry to kill? Do you love war?" Gorbash kneeled down beside the lone ugly as he held his head up to pour water down his mouth. Gorbash said to him, "You lived through the explosion, because you did not eat." The lone uglykind shook his head yes.

"Me di, me di ptse, me di," it said and passed out. Gorbash cut the uglie's stomach open and put a cooked fish inside, then closed it up.

The lone ugly sat up and started to cry, "No save me, no save me? I want die, no ugie no ugie, no ugie. I want die."

Gorbash lifted the lone ugly up to his feet, as he asked him, "Wouldn't you like to live with kindness—doing good for others and others doing good for you.?" The lone ugly sat back down, wrapped his four arms around his four legs, and started to cry heavily.

In between sobs, he told Theodore and Gorbash, "Hate me ugie, me help them run as ever could. Many time no eat." The lone ugly fell flat on the ground, folded his four arms across his chest, and told his two listeners "Help; help. Cannot, die, die." Gorbash explained to Theodore that the lone ugly wanted to die, that he had helped people run and he hardly ever ate. He would have liked to help people, but now he wanted to die.

Theodore said, "Let's grant his wish and kill him; that's my wish too."

"No!" yelled Gorbash. "No! He wants to do good; he is alive for a reason, and we will preserve that reason. The lone ugly will ride on the other side of you."

Theodore yelled back at Gorbash, "I want to kill him!"

Gorbash turned to Theodore with dismay in his eyes as he shot out a flame of fire in the air. "Theodore, you hateful creature, keep your mouth shut. This I say, and this you will surely do. I will tell you another thing, Theodore. Someday you will be grateful he lives. How would you have liked it if I had treated you the way you're treating him? Remember, I had a better reason than you do; he and his kind have never hurt you. Now, climb up and shut up—unless you would prefer to walk." Gorbash helped the lone ugly get into the other seat behind his ear and secured him. He didn't help Theodore get up. He told him, "Theodore, get up, and be done with it." Theodore scrambled to get into position, but he made it. Up Gorbash flew, confident because he knew that Theodore had needed the scolding, even though he hadn't liked scolding him. Gorbash flew straight for four hours without stopping. It started to rain and hail, so Gorbash took his two riders into an open cave for protection.

The three of them watched the scene with fascination from the cave's opening. A small, five-foot dragon swirled around and around in the air, spitting blue fire at the large balls of hail. He was kicking at the hail as he spat forth the flames. The small dragon was such a strange sight—Theodore could see right through his body to his bones, yet he had a remarkable kind of beauty. His movements were fluid, as though he were dancing. His eyes were yellow with one, long lone streak of black, and his scales were bone gray. This bone dragon posed no threat—it was as though he were calming down the storm. When the storm gave in, the bone dragon waved as he said, "A peaceful way is by way of a peaceful mind."

The lone uglykind tried to say, "Thank you, peace dragon Gorbash for saving me. If I lived for only this, I am happy."

Theodore excitedly said, "I could understand what he was trying to say. I knew what he said." Then Theodore softly told Gorbash that he was sorry for the way he had reacted to the uglykind.

Gorbash told Theodore, "I know you are really a good person.". The bone dragon was out of sight, and the storm was over. Gorbash and the riders were ready to put in some more cloud miles, but first they had to stop for food. Gorbash flamed some killer fish, and the others picked some wild bread fruit. Gorbash held the lone ugly and pushed some food into his mouth. He told him, "You have to learn to eat this way; I will help you learn." The lone ugly clapped his four hands and smiled at Theodore. Theodore was crying as he smiled back. Gorbash told Theodore, "Theodore you must be nearly out of your sustaining berries; you're welcome to eat hot fish and torn fruit bread with us."

Theodore told Gorbash, "I sure would like that, and I like the hot mayapple drink you made, Gorbash, thank you." Gorbash had tears in his eyes as he looked at Theodore and said, "Theodore, I doubt if I could ever be as proud of anyone as I am of you right now. You've made such a quick recovery." The lone ugly shook his head in agreement and was crying real tears, for the first time ever, and not puss. The ugly sat there shaking from the cold. Theodore tried to climb up to Gorbash's ear, when Gorbash took Theodore's bag out and handed it to him. Their eyes met for a minute, then they both smiled. Theodore got a blanket out of his bag and covered up the ugly.

The ugly said, "Never had a blanket." Gorbash and Theodore looked on in shock as the ugly hugged the blanket and fell fast asleep. Gorbash asked Theodore if he also wanted to rest. Theodore lay down on his brown bag, next to the lone ugly. The lone ugly put some blanket over Theodore. Theodore let him lay his head on some of his brown bag.

To share and care; how rich, Gorbash thought. Seagon stopped back for a while to talk to Gorbash.

"The night sky is so beautiful after a storm, isn't it Gorbash?" said Seagon.

"You got to see the bone dragon, didn't you Seagon?" asked Gorbash.

"Yes, I did see it from afar, and I m beginning to realize I am as much a threat to others as I think they are to me. I'm thinking of a lot of things," said Seagon.

Gorbash told Seagon, "So am I. So am I."

Seagon looked into Gorbash's eyes and said, "I get the feeling we are in for a lot of lessons, a lot of learning, and a lot of happiness."

Gorbash said, "You got it, Seagon; you got it." Seagon flew away to keep watch or to keep safe—perhaps both or neither. Gorbash thought to himself, *This one is nice, very nice, but there is something strange about the way he flies away in intervals.* Gorbash flew above Seagon to learn where he was flying. Gorbash knew the two riders were sound asleep.

Seagon flew to a large body of water, where a ship was resting at port. Gorbash watched him from above, trying to keep out of Seagon's sight. He saw Seagon hide when the seamen came aboard: some were knights, and some were not. When the captain got out to sea, Seagon came out of hiding. Seagon just stood there with his wings wrapped around himself.

He was watching—waiting for someone to make a move. All the humans ran down to the cabin except one small, dark knight. He said, "I will kill you deader than a skunk." The dark knight charged Seagon with a sharp sword, but Seagon swooped him up and ate him in one giant gulp. Seagon never bothered the others in the cabin down below. But Seagon had to regurgitate him up over the side of the ship. He was not interested in eating human flesh, but he was very interested in hating them.

Gorbash angrily picked up Seagon under the wings and took him to the shore. Seagon was yelling, "Put me down, you bully. You can give the order to kill, but I can't kill anyone unless he tries to kill me first. I could fight and kill you, but I don't want to. I saved a ship by pulling them to shore, and I've never eaten any who have not tried to kill me. One time I almost died from a stab in the chest. Just before I died, I ate my attacker and I lived. But I couldn't keep him down; I regurgitated him over the side of the ship. That is how my sea dinners began.

Gorbash said, "I don't know what to do with you."

Seagon said, "You eat killer fish, and you called me half fish, so why can't I eat killer knights?"

Gorbash answered, "But they're humans."

Seagon said, "No! They are not humans; I can't eat humans. But I can eat dirty, rotten killers. Do you call the ones who killed your kin 'human'? Some knights don't want to kill, so I leave them alone, but some love to kill—those are the ones on my menu. Do you want to stop me, Gorbash?" Seagon asked. "Then put a sword through my heart."

Gorbash said, "Seagon, I'd like to go with you sometime to see how you operate."

Seagon said, "Yes, that's fine, Gorbash. You don't approve of what I do, yet you want to check up on me. Just who are you, Gorbash? Are you the loyal order of the court? Or are you the simple joker? Gorbash," stated Seagon, "I don't approve of what I do, killing the rotten killers, but I sure don't approve of what they do—killing the sweet and innocent, over and over. Someone has to do something about it. Well, I am that someone. I have saved some sweet and innocent. I just wish I could have done something before ours had to die! I m going to fly away now. Kill me or let me go."

Gorbash told Seagon, "If I find your word cannot be trusted, just remember, I'm a killer-fish-eater. If you take this as a threat, you're correct: it is a threat. Tell me, what would you do? Your guess is as good as anyone's." Gorbash flew away, leaving the water dragon behind. He thought, *This new dragon can't trust anyone, but can he be trusted?* Gorbash flew back to the others with heavy thoughts. Gorbash didn't like what he saw. He was always looking for ways to save life, not take it. Gorbash cried big blue dragon tears as he flew back to the cave.

Chapter Twelve
A Dragon Fight

Gorbash received a transmission from another dragon named Stone. Theodore could hear what they were saying. The one named Stone said, "Gorbash you may be their leader, but you are not mine. You are older than I am, but you are not bigger. It is said you are strong, but I say you are weaker than I am. The dragon realm says you are the kindest of us all, while I find your kindness is your largest weakness. You live to preserve life; watch me as I take over all life and kill those who would dare to oppose me." Then the dragon laughed.

The transmission went dead, and Gorbash couldn't get Stone back. Gorbash thought sadly, *We have not heard the last of Stone. I feel the young dragon has a death wish. He is a very sick dragon—the only male of his kind. I will tell everyone what has made him such an angry dragon, but I'll wait until all the dragons have gathered.* After the two sleeping friends awoke, Gorbash put them in their safe place and flew up to get some cloud miles behind him, still thinking about Stone. Some of Gorbash's giant, warm, blue dragon tears splashed on a flock of birds flying by. They enjoyed it like a warm birdbath.

While in flight, Gorbash was transmitting to other dragonkind. He was communicating to a dragon named Blacksma. Theodore couldn't hear everything they were saying; a couple times he could see a big, green scale break away from Gorbash—it made a loud pinging sound as it flew off. Then suddenly Gorbash yelled, "Hang on; we're going down." Within seconds, they were on the ground. Gorbash put a protective shield around the two riders as he sat them carefully on the ground in some wild flowers. He told them to stay still. Suddenly, a black, velvety dragon appeared. The bottoms of his feet and hands were deep blue.

This new dragonkind had velvet scales; his underside was midnight blue, while his eyes glared a cavernous blue. He stood on his toes when he walked. This was the only dragonkind that wore a large tuft of black hair on the top of its head. The black dragon was fourteen feet tall and had a wingspan of fourteen feet. He stood face-to-face with Gorbash. When fire shot out of the black dragon's nostrils, they both flew up into the air in circles and slammed into each other.

The black dragon swirled downward, around and around to the ground, with Gorbash speeding down after him. He aimed his head toward the other dragon. Within seconds, Gorbash was on him, like bears on a honey pot. "I say now, Blacksma," said Gorbash. "It's time to act like a mighty dragon, not like a little wounded bird. Get up and fight like a real dragon." Gorbash let the black dragon up, and the black dragon flew high, until he could no longer be seen. Gorbash shot out red and yellow flames after him as a blaze of fire came falling down and hit the ground. The black dragon left a cloud of dust about half a mile around him. His beautiful velvet scales were singed and smoking, and the whites of his eyes were blood red. Gorbash—well, Gorbash looked like . . . Gorbash. He was unharmed.

Blacksma let out a vicious loud roar as he sprung to his feet with his wings fully spread. The black velvet dragon leaned his head back and laughed wildly. Gorbash spread his wings out too and laughed with him. "Ah, Gorbash, you're still the best. Now tell me, Sir Navigator, what do you have in the wind for the likes of me? asked Blacksma. Blacksma was walking around Gorbash in circles, with his wings folded behind him as he talked.

Gorbash put his foot out and tripped him. The black velvet dragon fell to the ground with a thud. Gorbash said to Blacksma, "Stand still when you talk to me." The mighty Gorbash went on to say, "All you youngins are alike; you have more energy than brains. Stay here; I have something to show you. Don't make a move until I tell you," Gorbash said to Blacksma. "Can you do that?"

"Yes, yes, I can do that. You know my word is gold, and my spirit is silver," uttered Blacksma.

"If that were true, would you have to announce it?" questioned Gorbash.

"Wow, you're so tough on me, my friend. Now what have you got to show me?" questioned Blacksma.

At first, Theodore dropped his brown bag to the ground and thought, "If my bag makes it, maybe I can make it." Gorbash leaned his head forward to let Theodore down, then Theodore slid down the dragon's back to the ground.

"What is this!" yelled Blacksma. "The great Gorbash carries ants now? Let me step on it."

"Blacksma!" said Gorbash as he folded his wing toward Theodore. "Let me introduce you to a humankind that has just saved my life. He calls himself Theodore."

Gorbash turned to Theodore and said, "Theodore, let me introduce you to a high-spirited velvet dragon named Blacksma."

Blacksma spit out black and red sparks as he told Gorbash, "You trust this speck of cosmic trash? Words mean nothing to them. You know they are sending our kind into oblivion."

Gorbash turned to Blacksma and said, "The dragon council has spoken; it is written on the Kaballa plates that a true heart will come to free us all; maybe Theodore is that true heart."

Gorbash turned to Theodore and said, "It's time to let the pain bury the pain; a bright new dawn will come upon us. We will live free or die trying; we must trust. Trust is all we have left."

Blacksma frowned as he spoke, "I will never trust the earth dung, but, mighty friend, I trust you, so tell me what you want Blacksma to do."

Gorbash looked at Blacksma and replied, "This is not a one-way road. As we learn to trust humankind, they must learn to trust dragonkind."

"On yes," yelled Seagon, appearing out of nowhere.

"What is this?" asked Blacksma. "Could this be a—"

"Don't say fish," said Seagon, "or I'll drown you where you stand."

"Drown me? Now that's a first," snarled Blacksma, "A dragon drowning me; I love it. I'd like to shake your hands, water dragon."

"Okay" beamed Seagon. "As long as you class me as a dragon, I'll shake your hand." But instead of shaking hands they hugged as they yelled together, "My long-lost cousin from Shangri-la."

So, off they flew toward their fate, with their big dragon hearts filled with hope and courage for a second chance at a new, safe way of life. After a few hours in the air, Theodore could hear Gorbash transmitting again, and down he swished to the ground, hiding Theodore behind a rock. Theodore watched as a small, white dragon emerged into the clearing.

Gorbash brought Theodore out to meet her. Her name was Pearl and she was delighted to meet Theodore. She said, "It's about time we reconciled with humankind. They misunderstand us, and we distrust them." Pearl asked Gorbash, "I heard the Onie tribe found him to be a true heart, isn't that a good start?"

"That's why I'm here, Pearl," said Gorbash. "It's high time we make a new start. Time will tell, but for some reason, I do trust this young member of mankind."

Pearl replied, "He has love written all over him—that much love can't be wrong."

Our lady dragon was a sight to behold. She had scales of pure pearl and real pearl adornments. Her voice was musical. She stood almost ten foot tall and had a wingspan of ten feet. The bottom of her small feet and hands were pinkest white, with little rips and tears. Her eyes were soft blue with a black streak in the middle. She walked as if she were floating on air, and maybe she was. The four dragonkind flew away together. Soon they were out of sight, and if a battalion of soldiers had been looking for them, they wouldn't have been able to see them, because they disappeared in the gray clouds.

Flaming Dragon Hearts: Pile cherry pie filling on top of a sweet tart. Pour brandy over it and light.

Chapter Twelve

AA

The day turned into night, and the glow of the moon lit the night sky for the four dragons. The four dragons began to cast strange, dark shadows across the night sky, like oversize bats. But they weren't bats; they were dragons. Morning came all too soon as they landed in an open meadow. They were making ready to meet another dragon. Theodore was a little nervous as he rested on a patch of wildflowers. He had no way to hide himself. While he was on his back looking up at the sky, he could see a large patch of deep red coming at him. The patch of red hovered two feet above him. The red dragon carefully picked up Theodore and spoke to him, "Aye—so you be the one all this fuss is about, just a damn bloody human. Maybe I'll drop you on your 'ead, aye, Laddie."

"No! No!" yelled Theodore, "Put me down. Gorbash," Theodore called, "get your pet to let me down."

"Aye," said the red dragon. "This one has nerves of rock for a wee little worthless bug."

"Put him down!" ordered Gorbash. "And be careful when you do; he's our reason for being here." Seagon came to meet him then flew ahead again; I guess you can say Seagon knew what was going on. The red dragon's name was Rednor. He was a beer-drinking dragon with a bad attitude. Rednor was thirteen feet tall and his wings spread to fourteen feet. His scales were blood-red; they spattered blood drops when he flew.

Rednor had a fast walk that jerked a little when he moved. His feet and hands were so red that they also left tracks of blood. Even his red eyes dripped blood. The word was that Rednor had way too much blood in his system, and it had to be released. The castle knights called Rednor a vampire and thought he sucked knights' blood. This wasn't true; Rednor gave blood but was unable to take it. Rednor's blood would match any blood, so Rednor gladly gave his blood to any kind that needed it. He respected Gorbash and saw him as a fierce leader, and he honored the old dragon. So off they all flew into the sky. They disappeared into the clouds and were out of sight. But Rednor didn't trust Theodore, not at all, in any way. He was watching him. Keeping an eye on Theodore became Rednor's mission.

Chapter Twelve
𝔅𝔅

When they landed, Rednor said in a husky voice. "That she-dragon, what's her name? Pearl! She has me in a dither. Seeing her made my heart jump out of my chest. I would like to make her me mate and have a wee little pup with her." Rednor's heart was outside his chest, thumping away; blood splattered in the air. He pushed his bleeding heart back inside his chest; as it went in, it made a loud thump. The next day, Blacksma and Rednor got into a fire fight. Theodore could see red and black swirling around in the sky. Flames lighted the clouds in rich colors of blue and yellow. In a matter of minutes it was all over, because Gorbash flew between them and tossed the two dragons to the ground. They walked away from each other grumbling with white sparks flying around them—a lifelong friendship gone because of a fight over a female dragonkind. Silly dragons. I guess they are male, are they not?

Pearl told the two dragons, musically, "Blazing dragons, why would you fight over me? You see, I have not met my mate yet. Please let the fighting end and become friends again." But Blacksma and Rednor walked their separate ways after that. Whenever they got close, they threw hot flames at each other.

Blacksma snorted at Rednor, saying, "What would a striking, rare and beautiful dragon such as Pearl want with the likes of a bloody dragon named Rednor?"

And Rednor spat blood back at Blacksma as he told him, "Aye, what would her sort of she-dragon want with the likes of a dragon with a wad of fuzz on the top of his head? Can thee tell me this?"

Gorbash tossed a barrel of ice cold water at Rednor and Blasksma as he told them, "This will cool both of you fools off. Don't you think it should be up to Pearl to choose? And she does not want either one of you. Now move it; we're leaving."

Rednor said, "Blacksma, look at Gorbash. He must think he's the boss or something, ordering us around like that. Maybe we should tell him to take a hearty leap in a shark-infested sea, don't thee think?"

Blacksma answered him by saying, "You know, Rednor, I think you're right. Let's get a hold of him and toss him into the sea of trouble. The thing is . . . Gorbash is the boss, and he can flip us together with both wings tied behind his back. Anyway, we are not as brainy as he is, and I love that darn big, old green dragon."

Rednor turned to Blasksma as he laughed out loud, "Gotcha, Blacksma. Laying all kidding aside, Gorbash can sure straighten us out in a hurry, and we are the better for it. I love that bossy dragon too." Then they said in unison: "That's why we're here. We know he's the very best of all the rest, and that includes us."

Seagon landed and asked the two dragons, "So you trust this domineering dragon?" The two dragons said, "We trust him with our lives and tails, and you will too when he saves your life." Seagon flew away without another word.

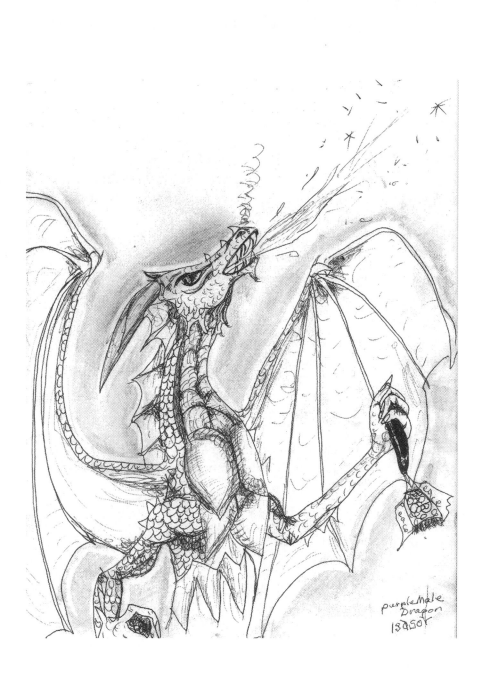

purple male
Dragon
13.05.05

Chapter Twelve
DD

Gorbash was behind Rednor and Blacksma while they had been talking, and he heard every word they said. Gorbash put his hands (if we can call them hands) on the red and black dragons' shoulders and told them, "I know you both are here because you want to be here, and you both know in your big dragon hearts that it is past time to make a great change for all concerned. Plus . . . I would like to take this time to tell you both how I really feel about you. Now get your long scaly tails off the ground and fly."

Blacksma turned to Rednor and asked, "Didn't Gorbash forget to tell us how he feels about us?"

Rednor looked back at Blacksma and said, "By golly, I know, he forgot to tell us how he feels about us—or did he forget on purpose?"

Seagon suddenly reappeared to the red and black dragons. He told them that he would be contesting Gorbash at the dragon tournament.

Blacksma said, "That sounds fishy to us, but if you think you have a chance, go ahead and try it. No one has ever defeated Gorbash."

Seagon growled and said, "Are you two calling me a fish? Rednor," Seagon added, "the knights say that you're a vampire. I don't see any reason for them to say that."

Then Blacksma said, "No! We would never call a dragon a fish; we eat fish. Sorry for the mistake." Blacksma said in a soft tone "You're our long-lost cousin, and we love you, cussy."

Seagon said, "Good, I feel like I'm loving you both too. I will watch over you to keep you safe."

Blacksma said, "Wow! How great is that, we have a bodyguard. We've been bodyguards, but we've never had one."

Rednor said, "By Jove, I've never had a bodyguard. I feel safe now, but I've never liked knights calling me a vampire. There's nothing to like about it."

Chapter Twelve

𝕮𝕮

The dragons flew up in the sky again, ready to travel. They wanted to cover some more cloud miles. Seagon flew with them; he was becoming more trusting. There was another dragonkind they had to meet up with. He was on his way; his name was Creighton (pronounced Krayten). He was a beautiful, iridescent white dragon. He stood fourteen feet tall with a wingspan of fifteen feet. He walked like he was on patrol, plus he was as fast as quick lighting. When Creighton landed, he spread his wings fully and stood on one foot—always on one foot.

Creighton was quite a handsome sight, at least that's what Pearl thought when his black-streaked blue eyes met her black-streaked blue eyes. It was love at first sighting. Oh, what a sweet, rare dragon-sighting indeed.

You could really say the sparks were flying. When these two met in the sky, they both turned shades of pink, then shades of blue, then shades of yellow, then back to all-white. "Ah! Dragons are a mighty sort, a mighty wonderful sort indeed," said Theodore.

When Blacksma and Rednor saw the two matches together, they both said, "Don't these two belong together? They sure look good up there." The two old friends vowed to never fight again, at least not over a female, but you never knew with them; they fought often. Gorbash let down the ugly and fed him fish, lots of different bread, fruits, and sweet berries. Then he slept.

They all watched as the two white dragonkind lit up the sky in beautiful fireworks of every color of the rainbow. They all watched except Gorbash. He sadly walked away with big, green dragon flooding the ground in his wake. When dragons take a mate, they take a mate for life, and only one offspring is born. If the mate or offspring die, that's it; there were no second chances. So you can imagine what the mighty Gorbash felt: sad and alone. Gorbash dried his eyes and told the others, "We have a special place to stop. We will stop at the cave of the teaching dragonkind." They flew above the clouds again until they reached the top of a tall mountain.

Gorbash yelled, "Dive down!" The dragons landed in a beautiful flower garden. In the distance they could see human children playing and laughing; they looked happy. Some of the teaching dragons were walking around between the children. Gorbash let Theodore down as Gorbash walked toward a deep purple dragon. Theodore followed him.

This teaching dragonkind was seventeen feet tall with a seventeen-foot wingspan. He walked with a limp, because his hip was hurt, and he spoke slowly and in a low voice. He was a heavy reader and wore small reading spectacles. Theodore asked Gorbash, "Where have all these children came from? Did these strange dragons kidnap them?"

"Surely not," replied Gorbash. "They saved them from vile kidnappers and violent parents. Once their educated and learn a trade, they can go wherever they want. Never again call these worthy dragons 'strange,'" Gorbash reminded Theodore.

Gorbash walked up to the majestic teacher dragon and said, "Glad to see you, Koreg. It's been ten years since last we saw each other. It was at the dragon tournament, but it's been good transmitting with you too." The dragon tournament took place every ten years. It was a chance for dragons to meet to view fire shows and to compete for status.

Koreg, who led the camp, told Gorbash, "Friend, I have two lavender dragons, male and female. They wish to fly with you and, hopefully, help free us." The lavender dragonkind had lavender scales and were blue under the scales. The bottoms of their hands and feet were also blue. They were fifteen feet tall with a fifteen-foot wingspan, and their eyes were deep purple. They walked with a skip. "Come now," said Koreg. "Let's have music, dance, and feast together."

Forty giant tables were put together and loaded with fresh water, killer fish, lots of flowers, fruits, flourless bread, fruit, and vegetables.

There were barrels and barrels of sweet brandy wine. This was food and drink fit for a king, or should I say, fit for a dragon—lots of dragons. The festivities went on long into the night, while the white dragons lit the sky with rainbows and fireworks.

Koreg and the watcher dragons could not leave the camp; they protected the children. Koreg started the camp when he saw a need to help children, and he had devoted his life to it. The two purple dragons were watchers but not mates. His name was Isasor and hers was Rythma, and they were ready to go with happy hearts. They all said their farewells as they readied for the trip.

Gorbash asked Seagon to lead the way as they flew in formation. They resembled a flock of geese, a flock of very large geese, indeed, except they were quiet, oh so quiet. Creighton and Pearl asked to leave the formation for a couple of days. Gorbash told Creighton, "Be sure to use your protective field so no one can see you."

"It is done," Creighton said cheerfully.

The two sweetheart dragons went to a crystal cave next to the cool dragon cove. The cave glowed from the colors behind crystals. It lit up the cave so beautifully. Creighton had been in the cave before, but this was Pearl's first time, and she was delighted with the splendor and beauty of it all. Pearl surprised Creighton by opening her chest wall and playing a golden harp on her ribs. She sang so sweetly that he fell back in a swoon of love. Wanting to reciprocate, Creighton did a tap dance, with bells ringing between each toe-tap. Pearl was so enraptured by his dance that she too fell into a love swoon.

The two sweethearts (as much as dragons can be sweethearts) held hands and drifted up to the glowing top of the crystal cave. Their love lifted them up to almost weightlessness as they sighed and cooed the night away. The colors of the crystals reflected off the whiteness of the dragons, who turned around and around like giant spinning coils, whirling somewhat out of control. Words cannot express the breathtaking beauty of the love in that crystal cave; you would have to have been there, then you would have fallen into a swoon of love too.

Chapter Thirteen
What Is It?

Gorbash said, "Follow Seagon, everyone. We have another special treat for you; it is someone I have met with off and on over the years. I'd like him to come with us on our journey." Down Seagon went with the others at his heels. They landed in a pasture with one giant tree in the center.

Theodore walked over to the tree and asked the others, "What are these deep scratches all up and down the tree trunk?"

Gorbash said, "Tell me, everyone, what does it look like?"

They all said, "It sure looks like a cat, a very massive wild cat, to be exact."

Gorbash lifted Theodore behind his ear, and Seagon told the others, "Dive now." In a flash, they were in an underground cave, an underground cave of remarkable elegance.

Suddenly they heard a strange sound, the sound of . . . purring, "What could that be?" the others asked.

Gorbash said, "What does it sound like?"

They all said, "It sure sounds like a . . . a cat, a very loud wild cat, to be exact." Suddenly they saw a shadow moving toward them—a very large, dark shadow. They froze in their tracks. Who ever heard of a dragon freezing in its tracks? But that's what happened. They froze.

Theodore peeked out from behind Gorbash's ear yelled, "Don't worry, you big, brave dragons! It's only a gargoyle."

"A gutter dragon, in fact," said Gorbash. "The word 'gargoyle' means to gargle. They were used for cleaning out cutters, but no one uses them anymore. Then they became town protectors, standing guard from the corners of buildings."

Theodore said, "I've read about them, just after I learned to read."

Gorbash said, "Step back away from the cave wall. I'd like you to meet my lifelong friend; his name is Asid."

Asid stepped into the light, and said. "Don't worry, my new friends. I cast a bigger shadow than what I am."

Seagon said, "He's as harmless as a dragon pup."

Asid was no more than five feet tall, orange in color, and had long, fat arms and short, fat legs. Asid had short wings that were dragon-like, but he resembled a cat standing up. He couldn't fly very high and not for very long. Because gargoyles have big, heavy feet and big, heavy hands, they don't have much flying power. The gargoyle Asid told everyone to come inside and dine with him, "We'll have a fancy feast," he assured them. The dining area was elaborately fancy with satin pillows around a low dining table. Asid had four cat-loving old women who waited on him, and they seemed to love him.

Theodore asked, "He has old women for slaves?"

Gorbash told him, "Didn't you ever hear of elderly ladies loving cats? Don't worry; they are only machines, with cat-loving built into them." They all sat around talking and laughing and each one took a nap on a satin bed. Then they washed, groomed, and proceeded to go to the dining area.

One of the machines got some birds out of a cage. She sat them on some sticky paper in the middle of the table. Another one got some killer fish out of a large fish tank and tossed them onto platters next to the birds. They all just stood there dazed, watching the fish flop around for a few seconds.

Smart Gorbash, not wanting to insult his friend, told the gargoyle as he rubbed his own tummy, "We have a long flight; could we get some to go?"

When they got away from the underground cave, Gorbash freed the birds, cooked the fish with his flames, and the two white dragons met them so they all shared the hot fish dinner. Pearl said, "So you visited your old friend, Asid?"

"Yes we did, Pearl," Gorbash answered.

"I was transmitting to you, and it seemed like you were in an underground cave; that's the only underground cave I know of," Pearl told Gorbash.

Seagon left as he said, "I'll remember what you told me, Gorbash. I have started to like this way of life."

Creighton turned toward everyone and said, "I have some cold cherry brandy; I kept it cold in the back of a cave: a five-gallon bottle for each one and a quart for the tidbit."

"Oh, thank you so much, big feller. I've never had a whole quart of brandy before," Theodore told Creighton.

Creighton replied, "That's okay, little buddy. You're the nicest member of mankind I've ever met. As a matter of fact, you're the only member of mankind I've ever met except when they tried to kill me, and they killed many a good friend," replied Creighton. Theodore drank his quart of brandy and fell fast asleep (or maybe slowly asleep) leaning against Gorbash.

Pearl said, "Look at him. Isn't he a precious human? Sleeping like a little dragon pup." They all talked and laughed while they drank their brandy, everyone but Gorbash, that is. He was staring at the ground.

"Ah, Gorbash, are you thinking about Asid?" asked Pearl.

"Yes, I am, Pearl. I should have invited him to go with us," said Gorbash.

"Datada!" bellowed both Rednor and Blacksma. "We can go carry him, by his arms, oh humble master," joked the two dragons. They both bowed to Gorbash.

Gorbash laughed, "Be on with you, then."

In two shakes of a dragon's tail, they were back with an excited gargoyle. "I knew it; I knew it," repeated Asid over and over. "I knew this big, old craggy dragon would not leave me behind." Asid danced around, singing and clapping. "I'm going to the castle; I'm going to meet a real king and queen, not a phony king like me," Asid said. "I knew you liked my fancy feast; that's why you dragons wanted me to come with you. I love it; I love it."

Rednor snapped at Asid, "Aye there, we didn't want your dinner, you fluffy fat cat."

Asid dropped to the ground, shrinking as he sobbed, "I hope I don't die of the shrinkles before I get to the palace. Will I die of the shrinkles, Gorbash?" Asid asked.

Gorbash told Asid, "No Asid, you won't die of the shrinkles, because I will ask Rednor to apologize, and then you will stop shrinking." Gorbash turned to Rednor and said, in a strong voice, "Rednor! Now that you have met my friend and ate his fish in friendship, you will apologize, or the fish of my friend will sour in your stomach."

Rednor went to his knees saying, "Ah! Me bloody words befall me, me buddy. Asid, aye, you need beat me on a rack and strip me, for it is I that shall live life in sorrow for the harsh words I've lashed at someone who has given me sup and lodging."

Gorbash had each member of the group tell Asid that he or she liked the food he had served. Each one said that while birds were not their favorite food, they had very much enjoyed the fish Asid stopped shrinking, and the dragons crowded around Asid as Pearl said, "Time for big dragon hugs."

Asid was so happy that he said, "Oh no! Now I will die of happiness."

"You will live of happiness," Gorbash told him. "We will all learn a valuable lesson, then . . . we will live of happiness," Gorbash reassured each one.

Seagon showed up to partake of the dragon hugs, and he said, "That all sounds good to me, and I would like to live of happiness too, with all you good dragons. We are a good lot, are we not?"

Everyone said, "Yes!"

Rednor fixed a strap on his back for Asid to use as he said, "Aye, me buddy, I'm to be your means of travel." Rednor looked at Gorbash and flashed a big red smile. Through his smile he winked and told Gorbash, "Oh majestic leader, thy greatest lessons I have learned have been from you. Tis you who taught me to be humble, and I have learned the true meaning of friendship."

Gorbash turned to Rednor and said, "Remember, as long as you shall roam this land, friendship is family, and if you have family, you have everything, so keep the friends close to your heart, for they can heal."

Seagon started to cry, "Gorbash, you sure are a remarkable dragon. Are you as strong as you are wise?"

Gorbash replied, "You'll be able to find out at the next tournament, won't you, Seagon?"

Seagon asked, "Can I beat you, Gorbash"?

"Dear Seagon," Gorbash said as he tilted his head slightly to the left. "If you have to ask, you must not be sure of yourself. Being unsure of yourself means you've lost already. Learn to be sure of yourself." The friendly dragons logged many cloud miles.

After a while, they spotted a beach and landed there to take a well-earned splash in the cool waters of Balltange just off the isle of Calistro. Asid was afraid of water, because of his heavy feet and hands. He was part cat too, so he stayed on the beach watching the happy swimmers. Just as Rednor looked Asid's way, he saw a jagged sand saw beast coming up through the sand and stabbing Asid. Theodore hit it with a rock, and it dried up, but Asid was bleeding to death; in the matter of a minute, he would be dead. Rednor, without giving it a second thought, ripped a large vein from his own arm and placed it in Asid's wound. Asid had lost scads of blood, but the blood

Rednor gave him did more than restore what had been taken. Rednor blew some flame on the wound; it healed, and Asid was well again.

But Rednor was spilling blood all over the beach, and he was quickly turning a pale blue. Theodore was already up to his neck in Rednor's blood, Blacksma had to hold Theodore up so he wouldn't drown. Gorbash screamed, "I will not leave him! A good deed must be rewarded, not punished." Gorbash took one end of Rednor's vein and tied it to the other end, and the bleeding stopped. But blood would never flow through that tied vain again. Gorbash thought, *Will he die because of the unused vein? Will it clot and kill him?*

These questions haunted Gorbash, then he watched the red hero get up to his feet as he pounded his chest and yelled, "Ne'er has me e'er felt so good. Gorbash, you have fixed my body; I bleed no more."

By tying off the vein, Gorbash had slowed the heart enough to pump less blood. Rednor shook Asid's hands as he told him, "Aye, me little buddy; you are looking good. What, with my rich dragon blood in your veins, now ye are my brother and I am your brother."

Then Rednor took a deep breath and turned to Gorbash with heavy, red tears falling from his eyes. Rednor stammered for words, *"Um, ah . . ."*

Gorbash told Rednor, *"Never mind, good friend. I know what you're trying to convey. Your eyes say it all."* The dragons were moved by the scene and stood in perfect silence. Seagon washed everyone free of blood. Then Gorbash called out to everyone that it was time to go. The mighty dragons had to shake the blood off their wings in order to get up off the ground. Seagon helped them with that too. But Pearl couldn't fly. She was deep in blood; it had grounded her.

Seagon washed her blood away. Seagon was a hero many times over. Creighton picked up Pearl as Rednor picked up Asid and Gorbash picked up Theodore. The ugly was already in place—Seagon put him behind his own ear. They all flew up into Seagon's spray. As his rushing waters washed the blood away, they all watched as Rednor's blood splashed upon the rocks, spilling out into the open waters and turning everything a deep, dragon red. Gorbash broke the silence by saying, "Seagon, you're a wonder, a great wonder of a dragon. Thank you; we are so glad to have you with us. Please lead the way." Gorbash thought, *It's over; it's done, and it's good, but now it's time to fly up and away into the sky.*

Both the lone ugly and Theodore yelled out together, "The majestic dragons—they are a beauty to behold; they help shape us and make us. We love them." Gorbash thought to himself again, *Oh, yes, it is wonderful. What great things one can learn from a mortal enemy, as I am gleaning this word love from humankind and dragonkind and back again.*

They were up above the clouds with Seagon leading the way, when Gorbash looked down. He saw twenty travelers riding horseback. They were the king's knights in armor, yielding dragon-bloodstained swords of death. Gorbash took Blacksma and Rednor down to talk peace with the dark knights. The threesome landed in a field about a mile ahead of the travelers. Gorbash spoke first: "Harness your swords, oh weary knights. We mean no harm."

Blacksma was second to speak: "As we were asked, we fly to the king and queen to build a trust and speak in peace."

Rednor was third to speak: "Aye, aye, thy fellow men. Wipe our blood from your swords and fear us no more; we come as your protectors."

One of the knights yelled, "Charge!" Creighton stopped his sword and landed on one foot with wings outspread, aglow with rainbow colors. The knight's blade went deep into Creighton's chest, and he fell with a thud. His lights faded, and the mighty dragon went gray. Pearl flew from the clouds to Creighton's side; within moments a blade pierced near her heart and her colors went gray too. Theodore quickly took out the magic potion from his bag. As he dumped it on them he said, "Would it work, or better yet, could it work? Please! Please! Let it work!"

The rest of the knights dropped their swords. With grim faces, they slid silently down from their saddles. The knights went to kneel at the side of the peaceful white dragons. Their dark knights' tears dropped down on the two dragons, whose white scales were falling to the ground. The two guilty knights took off their armor, tossed away their swords, and walked away in shame, screaming madly into the woods. The three remaining dragons, Gorbash, Rednor and Blacksma, wept. Oh, how the three dragons wept. Seagon flew down to weep with the other dragons; he stood beside the innocent knights that were crying. You could see no hate—just sadness for the loss. If you see a huge rainbow some day, perhaps it will be the tears of the four brave dragons. Gorbash created a protective shield to wrap around the knights for their long journey home.

Heads hung low, the knights and the dragons shared great sorrow that day. Would the two white dragons be spared by the magic potion? We will see; we will surely see. But our mighty Gorbash took Seagon away to walk in the woods the woods. He was looking for the two knights that had gone mad over their awful deed. When they found them, Gorbash and Seagon put them on their horses and told them they were forgiven, because of their sorrow. The two forgiven knightkind went with the other knightkind, but with warm tears still rippling heavily down their cheeks.

Gorbash told Seagon, "Oh, how forgiveness heals; it heals all the way around."

Seagon said, "Gorbash; I feel it myself. I love those white dragons. Let me take their place."

Gorbash spoke quickly, "No, no, Seagon. It is not your lot. Come with me, brave dragon." Gorbash returned to where the white dragons lay. Gorbash was there to protect the white dragons from further harm. Gorbash and Seagon drew back into the woods to watch without being seen; they had to lay on their sides covered with tree branches. It was not easy for a big dragon to hide from view, except in the clouds.

Within two hours, their waiting paid off. Two scrap buzzards arrived to pick up Pearl to scrap her pearls then feast on her remains. Here and there scrap yards were open for business, and Pearl's rare scales were going for a high price. Gorbash jumped from his hiding place, let out a high-pitched scream, and the two twin buzzards passed out from fear.

Seagon tied them up together and rolled them down a mountainside where they could wake up without knowing where they were. The two white dragons never lost their scales nor turned to dust, which meant that meant they were not dead. They were in a state of suspended sleep. Eventually, they regained their colors and flew to the castle with Gorbash and Seagon. Did the magic save them or not? Your guess is as good as mine, and I guess the magic was applied soon enough to save them from death. Now, what's your guess? Remember, your guess is as good as mine.

Gorbash thought it only right to transmit to the rulers of the castle, namely the king and queen, to warn them of the dragonkind who traveled to the castle. Gorbash shared each of their names with the king and queen and hoped for the best outcome.

Rednor's Blood Pudding: Take some red wine. Sweeten to taste. Thicken with cornstarch. It's a good, healthy pudding.

Chapter Fourteen, Part One
Meanwhile, at the Palace

All the dragonkind made it to the palace, with the knightkind not far behind. The dragonkind had watched from above, protecting the knights as they traveled. The dragons landed in the courtyard. When they looked around, they saw motionless human faces. Fearing their fate, they prepared to take flight. Then they heard hundreds upon hundreds of people cheering, "Gorbash, Gorbash, Gorbash," as the king and queen walked to greet them. The queen carried a sword—a tall, bloodless sword.

The king asked, "Which of you is the mighty Gorbash?" Gorbash stepped forward and declared himself. The queen placed her sword on Gorbash's shoulder and said, "Kneel, please. I knight you Sir Gorbash, the noblest of all knights."

Then the king asked Blacksma to step forward. The queen said, "Kneel, please. I knight you Sir Blacksma, a brave knight of the round table." The king asked Rednor to come forward, and the queen said, "Kneel, please. I knight you Sir Rednor, a hero knight among heroes." The king then asked for Isasor. The queen said, "I knight you Sir Isasor, the keeper knight of the castle lands." The Queen asked if Seagon wanted to be knighted.

Seagon replied, "Thank you, dear queen, but that is more than I can take; no knighthood for me, never!" Gorbash told the king and queen that Seagon was already a water dragon king.

The king and queen knighted all the male dragons. Gorbash whispered to the king, and the king asked Asid to come forward. Then the Queen told Asid, "Kneel, please. I knight you Sir Asid, a brave dragon-blooded knight indeed."

Asid walked around the courtyard, dancing and singing, "I am a brave dragon-blooded knight, a brave dragon-blooded knight indeed, so said the queen, and I will never prove her wrong. I say, the queen has spoken, everyone hear me out, the queen has spoken. Oh yes, the queen has spoken, and I will heed her words and never do her shame, oh yes, oh yes."

The queen stepped up to the stage on the big screen to tell all people, "This night we shall have a wedding, the wedding of our daughter to the true heart, Theodore. All are welcome to attend." The queen also said, "There will be food of all kinds, drinks of all kinds, people of all kinds, and yes, brave dragons of all kinds." The wedding went on for three days and two nights. Everyone loved, laughed, and made merry. From a palace window high up in a balcony, the king came to speak:"Ladies, gentlemen, and dragons, this marks a great moment in the time of this kingdom. You have been part of history.

"My *dream has been to* unite dragonkind and humankind in my lifetime. This wonderful *sight is better than I* had *ever dreamed. I'd like to thank the land named Alaska for the chunky gold rings that each dragon will receive. Its circle will be an emblem of everlasting trust between two deferent kinds that have become* so *much alike.*" Humans and dragons gathered in the courtyard to sing songs in the good king's name. For it was the king who had dreamed of uniting dragons and humans, and his dream had come to pass.

The dragons erected a sixty-foot flag that read, "To him we owe our freedom. King Kohler, the greatest king that ever ruled the land, a wise king that changed history; We honor him and his wonderful queen who stands at his side and rules with a strong, loving hand." The king and queen presented Seagon with a blue-gold jeweled crown. They penned a parchment to honor King Seagon, the great water dragon king.

web finns

Blow Hole

Extended jaw

← gills

wing wrap

web feet + Hands

Seagon
male water Dragon

Chapter Fourteen, Part Two
The Days of the Tournament

The tournament was held on castle grounds. Dragons attended from all over, wearing their best dragon finery. The king and queen erected a stadium for human spectators. The knighthood changed as a result of its bad, bloody past—a past that held so much death for the dragons. The king and queen thought it only fitting that the dragons became head knights. The humans did not disagree, realizing that they needed balance to retain their new partnership with the dragons. Seagon was the announcer; everyone loved his voice, because he sounded like he was talking under water. Seagon asked that his name be withdrawn because he knew he could beat Gorbash.

Gorbash said, "On no, we must lay this question to rest. Can you beat me? I will never withdraw my name from a tournament. It is only fair that everyone has a chance to win."

So Seagon yelled over the loudspeaker, "Let the games began, so I can win!" The food was brought in; the brandy set in place. The dragon guards took their posts. There was a long line of dragons waiting to challenge Gorbash. And Gorbash stood alone. The fire lights were going off, and humans were dancing. There was lots of singing, lots of dancing, and lots of everything.

The arena was marked off for the fights. Gorbash took on the long line of challengers, sometimes five and six at a time. One yellow-and-orange dragon threw giant balls of fire, but Gorbash tossed them back at him. One brown dragon threw piles of mud, but when Gorbash flamed it, it turned to sand that the children could play in. The hours went by, but Gorbash never tired. The human spectators cheered for Gorbash. His dragon friends cheered for him too. The last dragon stepped up to challenge him; it was Seagon. Seagon told Gorbash, "I know now for sure I can take you." Seagon bowed twice to the people.

The people and dragons were quiet. Just at that moment, Seagon blew out a large shot of water like a huge fire hose; it tossed Gorbash to the back of the arena. Gorbash stopped himself, stood up, and told Seagon," I was ready for your water power. Are you ready for my lightning power?"

Seagon said, "I can take anything you have." He opened his mouth to blast more water at Gorbash. Gorbash shot him with blue bolts of lightning power that hit the water, and it lit Seagon up like the starry night sky.

Seagon was out like a burned-out firefly; smoke rolled off the top of his head for two hours. Seagon did recover, a little burnt, a little blistered, and very much embarrassed. Seagon told Gorbash, "I didn't want to fight you because I liked you, and I thought for sure I could beat you. I didn't even know what happened; I guess you're what happened. Gorbash, I am a better dragon because of you in every way; I give you thanks," and he bowed to Gorbash.

Gorbash told Seagon, "No need to bow to me, Seagon. I only did what I had to do, and it is over now."

In the days that came to pass, much happiness filled the castle, the grounds, and all around. Theodore saw Gorbash with his head down. He walked up to the mighty dragon and said, "Say, my best friend, I have something for you." Theodore was dragging a rather large cart behind him, It was covered with a brown tarp much like the brown bag of Theodore's trip. Theodore pulled the tarp off to reveal two green dragons: Marta and Yagoo. They jumped out of the cart.

Gorbash said, "Ugh, no! They are gone! They are ashes in the wind; they are no more," and he turned to walk away, sobbing profusely.

"Gorbash!" yelled Theodore. "The scales you saved. I cloned them from that, let the dead bury the dead, but let the living live on. They are alive! It is them—bone of bone, scales of scales, and memory of memory."

Gorbash turned to Theodore and said, "Oh, Theodore! What have you done?" Gorbash's cloned family ran to him crying with joy. Yagoo told Gorbash, "Father, I am so happy to be with you and mother. Oh, happy day; oh, happy day."

Gorbash turned to Theodore and said, "From now on, you shall be known as Theodore the unwise."

Tears flooded the ground as they splashed around in it—tears of joy and tears of apprehension. Theodore asked Gorbash, "Why haven't you cloned them before? I know you know about cloning, and why call me unwise?"

Gorbash looked at what looked like his family and said, "Remember when I told you some things may be better not knowing?"

"Yes, I do, but what did you mean?" asked Theodore.

Gorbash frowned and said, "Now you ask. Why didn't you asked before you did this? Cloning is copying. Marta and Yagoo are dead," replied Gorbash. "Maybe they wouldn't want to be copied—did you ever think of that? I sure wouldn't want to be copied. Every copy contains defects. Yet, whatever that copy does will reflect on the original. Would you want a defect acting out in your name? You should have asked, oh, foolish boy. I would have said no." Gorbash put his head down as he said, "I cannot destroy them, but it is vain to want to hold onto a copy and say it is real. Theodore, do you think I am vain?"

Gorbash said, "Now, I would tell you cloning is good. Yes, I say cloning is good. It helps to recover a part that is failing. It gives someone back his sight. It repairs what is broken. It can even, if a being so chooses, create a new body. Now there is a way to put someone's brain in a robot, but that life would be mostly, robotkind, not humankind Or dragonkind. I pity the creature; sooner or later, it would go insane."

Gorbash went on to say, "Theodore, cloning cannot bring back the original. Only bits, pieces, parts, and some memories of the original."

Theodore looked so sad, but he lifted his head up as he turned to Gorbash and said, "Gorbash you're so wise about doing the right thing; maybe sometimes you're too wise. These two may not be them, but a likeness is better than nothing, isn't it?"

Gorbash never said a word; he just shook his head.

Seagon told Theodore, "Please Theodore, can you clone my mate and offspring?" Theodore asked Seagon if he had anything of them. Seagon said, "I have their webbed fingers, is that all right?"

Theodore told Seagon, "That is perfect; let's get to work." Theodore turned toward Seagon, "You do know they will only be copies, and you can't change your mind."

"I know, I know!" Seagon said. "Like you said, Theodore, it's better than nothing." Seagon got his wish in time—he had a family, his lost family. Seagon changed his diet, he ate crabs and lobster, bread, fruit, nuts, and veggies. He stopped eating humans, although at times he thought about it when he met a bad human, but he didn't hurt anyone. Seagon knew he couldn't keep them down, anyway.

Chapter Fifteen
And The Night Showed a Million Rainbows

That night; the sky glowed like a million rainbows as two white dragons threw colored sparks for all to see. It is said that a white dragon pup named Haze roamed the courtyard. He danced on one foot while a human girl named Breeze gave him sealing wax (to wax his scales) and lots and lots of other fancy dragon pup stuff. Breeze was a wonderful girl; she knew wrong from right. If she saw someone mistreating another creature, she felt sad and took steps to correct it. If you visit the castle any time, any day from this day forth, you will meet a boy named Jackie, who had his own little dragon named Puff, and she is pink in color.

Jackie and Breeze are the king and queen's grandchildren. Can you guess who the parents are? Yes, Theodore Payper and his wife Celia are the proud parents of Jackie and Breeze. Gorbash made a giant roller coaster in the palace yard; oh, what fun for everyone. The wee people and the fairies were brought to the palace. Gorbash took concepts from the future, such as hospitals run by dragon-knight-doctors. Female dragons became helpers (nurses). Gorbash also brought universities with all kinds of education and peaceful learning.

Some of the dragon knights were teachers. The lone uglykind worked to help people to understand that different wasn't really bad—just different. Soon the lone ugly became two-legged and two-armed, and happiness filled him. He became known as Teach. Some of the humankind taught and worked beside the dragons. Other dragonkind arrived and signed the treaty. Oh, yes, there were some issues to be dealt with, but for the most part, the treaty was a good thing.

An alliance was extended to all people outside the castle area. The dragons kept the peace. Gorbash found defects in Marta and Yagoo. Marta couldn't remember her death and didn't think she had died.

Yagoo had lost his other mind-speaking abilities that Gorbash had taught him; there were also things he remembered that had never happened. He always asked, "Where am I?" Marta hardly spoke and cried a lot. Gorbash thought, *I will always miss my Marta and Yagoo, for I know they are truly dead, but I cannot be mean to these two copies.*

The Gypsy named Gypsy came to visit the castle. She read the crystal ball and stayed twenty years. Fillip, her horse, came with her, and he was free to roam the palace yard. Fillip gave children rides, and he was so happy, happy, happy. The Onies came to visit and had everyone walking on hot coals. Who would have known there could be so many true hearts? The bare butt tribe came with their bean fruit; they all had a jumping good time. The green man was there with his neon jumping boots on, and a pair for everyone else. The women machines from Asid's cave came to help, and they sure did. All the nice people/ animals Theodore met on his dragon hunt came to visit in due time; many came to stay and help.

Just then, at that moment Theodore got hit in the head with a javelin and fell down on his back. Everything went totally black.

Chapter Sixteen
One Hell of a Dream

Theodore awoke on a Monday at ten o'clock in the morning with a pounding headache that wouldn't stop. He meandered over to his first-aid chest to reach for a pain reliever. After putting two dots on his forehead, he started to feel better. Theodore sat down on his red, sharkskin davenport that came up from the floor and reflected on the dream he'd had the night before. He pointed to his universal remote that was hooked to the davenport, and the news appeared on his eighty-five inch sunken wall television.

The robot news reporter was talking about a foiled tele-safe robbery, a sky train derailment, and an alien space crash. A robot meteorologist went on to talk about the weather. Theodore thought, *Why do they talk so much about the weather? Here in the city it's always seventy-two.* Theodore turned off the remote by pointing to it. He got to his feet and went to the food area to have the robot make a cup of hot cherry brew.

The robot took out a veggie-layered wafer from the dry freezer and placed it in the micro-blazer for two seconds as Theodore sat down to his crystal- and nickel-plated table to eat the wafer and drink the brew. He got to thinking of the strange dream he'd had, as he spoke out loud, "What a hell of a dream I had last night: talking dragons, me walking through a mountain, and a very beautiful princess."

Theodore looked around his house at all the wonderful possessions he was able to afford. He had a good job as the owner and editor of a leading telecaster business and led a relatively happy single life. A surge of loneliness ran through him like a bolt of lightning.

Theodore sighed as he thought, *I'd give everything I have to be with that beautiful girl and talk to that big dumb dragon.* Theodore got up from his fancy table as he poured the rest of his brew down the drain tube. "What a hell of a dream," he said to again.

Theodore told the robot, "You have the day off."

The robot replied, "That does not compute; that does not compute." Theodore snapped his fingers twice, and the robot went silent. His tele-aid, which was hooked to his ear lobe went off. It meant he had a connection from someone. He answered it by saying, "Okay, you have me, so talk." It was an employee from his telecaster business calling about a job change. He made the change for her then he disconnected by saying, "Tele-aid, off."

Theodore walked over to the window, taking a good look at his new air-Pod which had replaced automobiles. His air-Pod was outside and encased by a protective dome. "Easy travel," he said out loud. "Easy everything; that's what life is like. Look at this," he said as he walked around. "We have biodegradable clothes, wear them, then put them in a bio-deteriorater. I'd like to tell the people in my dream," he blurted out, "about the pets we have. If you feed them, they stay around; if you don't feed them, they disappear."

Theodore got sad as he said, "I had a big, beautiful Irish setter. I only forgot to feed her twice and I could hear her from afar, barking for me as she left. I cried for her for a long time. I thought a pet would keep me company, but I was gone so much." He felt buzzing on his ear lobe; it was the tele-aid. The person on the other end said, "Turn your vision on; I have mine on, so you can see me as we talk."

Theodore said, "No! I do not care to see you; I know what you look like."

The guy on the other end said, "You'd better go ahead and turn it on. I don't like to talk to someone if I can't see his face."

Theodore remarked back, "Well, I don't really care if you like it or not." Then he said, "Tele-aid off." Theodore felt so good about his confrontation, because this guy had always been a control-freak to everyone. The guy connected back, but Theodore swiped the tele-aid with his tele-card, and the guy couldn't connect back.

Theodore moaned "Oh! If I could only go to sleep tonight and wake up living in my dream, I'd be the happiest man alive." Theodore didn't have a companion. He thought it was because he was middle-aged, homely, and fifty pounds overweight. Even with all the plastic surgery, he still thought he didn't look good. Actually, it was because he lacked confidence in the dating arena. In his dream he was young, handsome, and slim, but he still wasn't a forward guy. The girl in his dreams had to court him, but he was mostly a good person in everything else.

Theodore sloped down in his davenport with a sad face contemplating what he must do to get himself out of his awful mood. He thought, *How can a person have so much of what he doesn't want and yet have nothing that he does want?* Just then he said out loud, "Why did I think I wanted all these *things?* They are just things, and it's like I want more, because I thought more might make me happy, but it doesn't." Theodore thought about his dream, as he said aloud, "I want that girl in my dreams to hold and to tell her I love her as she says 'I love you' back and . . . and children to call me 'Daddy.' Darn it, I won't go back to work anymore. I will just fade into the wood work; that's what I'11 do." He was so sad he cried as he slid down to the floor and onto his back.

Chapter Seventeen
I Can't Believe My Eyes

Just then he heard a loud commotion. People were running everywhere; there was lots of screaming and yelling. Theodore walked out to the street to take a good look. When he saw it, he couldn't believe his eyes. A big green dragon was plundering the streets. The dragon let out a loud roar as he threw red and yellow flames into the sky, causing white smoke to billow up way above the clouds. Theodore didn't know why, but he wasn't scared; he wasn't scared at all. Could he be hallucinating? Could he be dreaming again?

The big green dragon reached out to Theodore as the smoke strained through his teeth and said, "Come with me, oh little wart. You need to come home; this here is only a dream." Theodore didn't move; he was frozen in his tracks. He thought, This is what I wanted, but can I give everything up? All that I've worked for? The dragon repeated, "Come, Theodore, this is just a dream. Do not hesitate. You will lose your chance and be stuck in between the two worlds—the false and the real." Theodore ran and didn't look back. After all, in his dream, he had trusted the dragon. Gorbash leaned down so Theodore could crawl up behind his ear.

As they flew to the castle, Theodore looked back and saw that the city was disintegrating right before his eyes; everything turning to dust. Theodore yelled as loud as he could, *"Gorbash, you big dumb dragon, I love you for real."*

Gorbash yelled as loud as he could, *"Theodore, you little twit, I guess I love you for real too."*

Readers, please don't think this is the end of our story, for it isn't.

Meanwhile Back at the Palace

Gorbash and Theodore arrived at the palace in moments. Theodore said, "Gorbash how did we get here so quickly?"

Gorbash told him, "You hit your head and were in a deep dreamlike coma. All I had to do was awaken you."

Theodore asked Gorbash, "But but—"

Gorbash told Theodore, "I couldn't force you. You had to agree to awaken, and I only had seconds myself, or I would have been trapped with you in between the worlds."

Theodore was so moved by the fact that Gorbash had risked his life for him. He was crying as he said, "Gorbash, you took such a chance to save me. Thank you so much."

Gorbash told him, "At the risk of sounding corny, I'll say that I know you would have done the same for me, and you have. When a window opens on chance, you have to take it right then. That's all I did. But you're welcome."

Theodore kissed Gorbash on the knee. "What was that?" Gorbash asked.

Theodore said with great happiness. "That was a kiss of love."

Gorbash told him "Then you'd better go give that to someone who is awaiting you." Theodore ran up the castle steps as fast as he could in search of Celia, his dream girl. When he got to the top of the steps, he could see Celia being carried out the window by a very large red bird, and she was crying, "Theodore, help me!"

Theodore yelled back, "I will come and get you, my love." He ran down the steps right to Gorbash.

Gorbash told him, "Yes, yes, I know; we prepare to free her. I have an idea where the red bird is taking her." Gorbash went on to say, "That so-called bird is the last of its kind; I will not kill him, but I will send him back where he came from, never to return." Gorbash called

Rednor and Blacksma to come with him, but he told Theodore, "You cannot go with us. It's too dangerous for you; we must go alone."

Theodore asked, "What is that thing? Will my love be safe?"

Gorbash told Theodore, "Met bird! It only takes the regal so he can make slaves of them. Chances are he has others, and we will free them, also. He is a toothless birdkind; he won't eat the living, though he will eat the dead, but he mostly feeds on dead fish."

"What is his name?" Theodore asked.

"Pterenodonkind," answered Gorbash. "I will tell you more when we get back, I'll need a net to carry the captured ladies in."

Soon they were in the air as Rednor yelled back, "Aye, we will bring them all back if we live."

Blacksma said, "This bird is only six feet tall, but his wingspan is thirty-five feet, and that scares the scales off me."

But Gorbash bravely said, "We are dragon knights, so have no fear. We will return, and he will not come back here." Soon, they were out of sight making more cloud miles.

Chapter Eighteen
The Hideaway

The three dragons traveled nonstop for two hours. They were tired and hungry when they settled down on a corn field; they tried not to eat too much. The dragons walked a few miles to get a drink of water at a pond. Then they flew up and away in search of the Pteranodon's hideout. Within minutes, Gorbash said, "There it is; let's go down."

Rednor said, "Aye aye, friends. "We be in trouble; the opening 'tis small for our big bodies."

They found the cave's opening, and it was only ten feet high and forty feet wide.

"What are we going to do?" Blacksma asked.

Without saying a word, Gorbash flew up to the top of the cave, which was fifty feet high. Within moments, they opened a skylight that exposed the cave's interior. To their surprise, the bird was not there, but three ladies were dressed in maid attire and sitting together in a corner. Blacksma wondered, "What happened to that bird? Do you think he flew away because of us?"

"No, no he wasn't here to start with, or he would have come out when we landed," Gorbash told him. "If he was fearful, he would not have traveled boldly to the palace grounds and taken a captive."

"Where can he be?" both the red and black dragons asked.

"There's only one place he can be: at a nearby castle taking another captive," Gorbash told them. Just at that time Pearl landed to pick up the ladies. She safely put them in the net and flew off to the castle. One of the dragons flew behind her to make sure she was safe. He was gone about an hour as they waited for Pteranodon to return to his cave.

Rednor and Blacksma noticed Gorbash takeoff into the sky. They saw the big red bird coming right at him. The Pteranodon dropped the lady he was carrying, and Blasksma carefully caught her and placed her on the ground safely behind a large bolder. Pearl came and picked up the lady.

Gorbash knew he could beat the bird in a fight, but he also knew he could not out-fly him. This one-of-a-kind bird was light, with a smooth, wide wingspan, which meant that he could fly fast and long, but he was no good on land. Dragons, on the other hand, were heavy and had a shorter-scaled wingspan, causing them to be slower in the sky than the bird but stronger on land.

The Pteranodon had no intention of allowing himself be caught by the strong dragons, so he screamed a high-pitched scream, "To the queen I go; she's mine," he said and off he flew toward the castle. And the three dragons had no intention of allowing him to reach the castle. After all, they protected the palace and humankind. They were dragon knights of the castle, and they would protect it at any cost. But what were they to do? They could not catch the red bird. Gorbash had a quick plan that he shared with the other two dragons. He told them to take a deep breath and blow out hard and long at each side of the red bird. Gorbash took to the middle as he waited for the two dragons to do their job.

Red and yellow fire shot out reaching each wing of the red bird, slowing him down. Then Gorbash blew out white fire to the middle while he grabbed the bird's feet. The three brave dragons carried him playback to his place of origin. The bird was a disturbed mutant descendant of the flying dinosaurkind, and the dragons had evolved from the landed dinosaurkind. The three dragons put the angry red birdkind down and told him, "You did this to yourself by taking humankind captive. Now go and harm no more." As they flew away, they could see the bird would never be able to fly again, and that made Gorbash sad. The bird would always be one-of-a kind, and now others would be safe from him. At least he was alive, if grounded.

Rednor and Blacksma were singing as they put some cloud miles behind them. The three proud dragons landed on a beach to dine on some berries, fruit bread, nuts, and killer fishkind, when they heard this strange ticking noise. As they looked up, they saw a huge black cloud overhead flying right for the castle. Gorbash told the other two dragons, "It's the locusts. They are two feet long, and they eat everything in sight, including each other." Then he went on to say, "That is why they have to fly so fast, so the ones behind them won't eat them."

Rednor asked, "What would there be done to our people if they reach the castle?"

Gorbash answered, "I just told you, they will eat *everything* in sight."

The red and black dragons cried together, "What can we do? Oh great leader, what can we do?"

Gorbash answered, "The only thing we can do to stop them is to burn them alive, or I should say, burn them dead." Gorbash said it sadly.

Blacksma told Gorbash, "We are injured, because we injured the red bird, but if we kill, we will surely die."

Gorbash told them, "We have to give our lives for the lives of everyone at the castle, and we must do it fast, without any more thought of ourselves." The three mighty dragonkind started crying like babies as they torched the locusts, saying together, "We are protectors of the castle; we can't kill, but we must learn to kill to save the castle." The flames burned red and yellow until all the locusts fell to the ground in a heavy heap of ashes and dust. The flames ended in smoke as the dragons looked hopelessly at what they had just done. They were suspended in mid-air for moments, not moving at all.

Soon the three dragonkind started to lose scales as they began to fall from the sky. Downward they went, spiraling around and around as they thought, Taking life is awful, but saving life is nice. The dragons' descent slowed; something was underneath the dragons, bracing them.

It was Creighton, Pearl, and Isasor. They softly lowered the dragons to the ground. Pearl said in a singing voice, "Brave knights, you should not suffer death for saving the castle grounds and its inhabitants. Yes, you have killed, but only in defense of thousands of humankind. You have saved your former enemy at great cost to yourselves."

Then Creighton chimed in to say, "I think and then think again; we are knights now, and we are to live different lives. We make decisions we never could have made before. The killing ban that was upon us is lifted, for we chose to forgive our enemy. By that act, we learned to love them and chose to die for them. In fact they love us, even as they love each other. Now get up and fly, and you will grow bright new scales."

Gorbash said, "Creighton, you are wise. Thank you for your quick wit."

Chapter Eighteen
The Story of the Frog and the Dragon

Up they all flew together as a group, but Gorbash said in a soft voice, as soft as a dragonkind could talk, "Let us three go down to the ashes and pay our respects to the life we ended."

Each dragon spoke these words, as they hung their heads low: "I wish it could have been different, and some day it will be; we are here to see to it." Up they flew to the others, and the six honorable dragons flew in formation.

They didn't say a word before they reached the castle. People were cheering their return. Gorbash thought, *How could they cheer? The dead cannot cheer; they cannot laugh; they cannot love; and they cannot understand why I took away every single thing from them—their breath, their life, their all. I, the so-called Gorbash, the one they say knows all, I gave the orders to take it all away and leave them nothing. We must learn to find another answer. Death is not an answer; it's too permanent, and nothing is learned in death.* Just then he saw a frog that hopped in his path.

Gently Gorbash picked up the frog and said, "Little frog, you kill to live, and others kill you to live, and I kill killer fishkind to live, and there have been those who have tried to kill me for fun. I have no liking to kill you; I have no liking to kill at all." The frog jumped out of his grasp and said, "Right it, right it, right it," and he swam away out of sight.

Now Gorbash knew what he had to do, and he learned it all from a little frog he would not kill. He had to go to his cave alone in solitude until he learned the answer. The king had awakened early and was standing on the balcony. He saw and heard everything that Gorbash was saying. Gorbash was standing face-to-face with the king. The king said to Gorbash, "Kindness lingers forever in the hearts of the good, Gorbash. You go to plant a seed of knowledge, and we will reap your harvest when you return. It is what you want to do, because it is who you are—the mightiest of the mighty and then some. I will let everyone know where you have gone and why.

We will await your return."

But Gorbash didn't hear the last part because he was out of view, on his journey to discover the best of himself in order to make himself better for all—and he met *all*. The king thought out loud, "Doesn't it feel good when someone helps you to see clearly and you can live and give the kindness to another? It's better than forgetting each other to judge one another harshly. It means so much to have someone care—really, really, care. It takes a dragon to teach us all how to be human, and most of all to be kind."

The king blew the trumpets, sounded the horns, and rang the bells. He came to the forefront on the screen and told the people of Gorbash's heavy heart. He said, "Gorbash may very well be the greatest beingkind that ever lived. Gorbash is hoping everyone will learn to honor life—to save life instead of taking it." People began to understand that if their life was precious to them, so were other lives precious, and it is better to help others understand too.

Theodore told the people that, "I found out by living with them that dragonkind are a wonderful sort, a wonderful sort indeed."

Pearl
White singing Lady Dragon

Chapter Nineteen
Alone in His Cave, or Was He Alone?

Gorbash returned to his cave, opened the skylight, and then closed it, but the light stayed bright. Gorbash felt someone watching him, but he couldn't see it. Still, he knew someone was there. The fairies were at the castle; the wee people were at the castle too. The giant roller coaster was turned off, and everything was quiet. Everything except whatever it was that was following him around and watching him. Gorbash got a little creepy feeling, and he had to realize, *I'm a big, brave dragonkind, or* at *least I think I am.*

Then he thought, *Maybe I'm a cowardly dragon, but I will find out, soon.* As he walked around, he started talking to himself, "What or whoever you are, come out in the open and show yourself." Then he said a little louder, "Do you have good intentions or bad intentions?" Gorbash heard a clicking noise, and it got louder and louder. The clicking followed him around. Gorbash yelled again, "Tell me—no, are you of a good kind or of a bad kind? Tell me."

The voice of many voices came back at Gorbash, What do you know about good intentions? You killed a whole village just to save another village." Before Gorbash could speak, the voices said, "What gives you the right to make that decision?"

Gorbash yelled, "I gave myself the right to save a village from deadly attackers. The village appointed us as their protectors. I feel sad about the death of all the wild locustkind, but I also feel gladness about saving the good villagers."

The voices yelled back just as hard, "They kill because they're so hungry; it was food to them. What gives you the right to take their food from them and give them death instead?"

Gorbash blew out a long flame of fire as he flew up into the air. He told the voices, "This is what we were built for, to be protectors.

But we pledged a long time ago to die if we took life." He came down again and told the voices, "Now you give us reasons to doubt ourselves, to doubt our very lives, to doubt our very source."

The voices asked him, "So you are rethinking things. Do you think one life is better than another?"

Gorbash snapped at the voices, "One life is not better than another; I think it is all about saving life; some living beings do not care about life. If I had let all the kingdom die, would that have made me a better dragonkind? But I'm a killer, yes, I know, and I feel torn about that."

The voices said, "Oh, greatest dragon, no matter which choice you made, you would have felt torn." Then at that very moment, seven spirits clad in locust bodies showed themselves in a mist as they told Gorbash, "We were testing you, good dragonkind. We as locustkind are evolving into farmers. Someday we will only grow our food, and it will slow us down, because our metabolisms are so fast, so we eat what is in front of us. You must know that you only did what you had to do, big feller. You helped, so we could evolve into right beings."

Gorbash put his head down as he said, "If I did the right thing, then why do I feel so bad? And why am I making excuses for myself?"

The voices told Gorbash, "It is who you are. You will teach the value of life and continue to do what you have to do." The mist left as the voices said, "Other spiritkind will be at your side from time to time and let their voices fall on your ears."

Gorbash decided to return to the palace, but this time he had a different frame of mind, and he knew what he had to do. He thought out loud, "So, I will be teaching the value of life. I feel good about that—I feel real good about that." Off he went to the palace to start his new life, hoping he would be able to fulfill his mission to the utmost.

Chapter Twenty
Back to the Castle

When Gorbash returned to the castle, he found things very quiet. People walked around with their heads hanging down and sad expressions on their faces. Gorbash went right away to his side cave to see his cloned family; maybe they could tell him what was wrong with everyone. But when he approached them, they had long faces too. Well, they were as long as dragon faces can get. Yagoo went to Gorbash, jumped in his arms, and told him, *"The beautiful queen is on her death bed and calling for you. Oh, father, whatever are we going to do?"* Gorbash went to the queen, bent down beside the king, and held the queen's hand as he told her, "My Queen, I must tell you that I will find the problem, and you will heal."

The queen told the king, *"Do not clone me, but clone my illness if you can. I must sleep now."* Gorbash went to the garden grounds where all the wee people and fairies lived. Gorbash lay down on his side on the plush garden grass. I know you know that dragonkind cannot lay on their backs, because of their wings. Gorbash tried to reach the ancient mindkind in hopes that they would give him an answer that would save the queen. But nothing came. He asked and asked, and then something came to mind. Gorbash thought, *How marvelously strange that sometimes things come to mind, and other times, there's nothing.*

But what came falling on his ears and mind was that a sourkind crawled by way of the queen's ear canal and that it soured some of her brain cells. He needed to get a sweetkind to stay on the outside of her ears to tempt the sours to come out. Then he would put the sours safely out into the deep woodland. So Gorbash had the humans look for the sweets with rubber gloves. They placed them on the outside of the queen's ear, and the sours came out. Once this happened, Gorbash placed both the sweetkind and the sourkind in the woodland to balance each other out.

The queen's ears were red for a while, but she fully recovered. Gorbash stated, "Insects are needed in many ways for many reasons, and yet every ten seconds a person dies of malaria, a disease carried by certain mosquitoes. Half of all human deaths throughout history were caused by mosquitoes. Other insects can and do carry diseases that kill both humans and animals. Also, insects are many times stronger than humans; humans have six hundred muscles while many insects have four thousand separate muscles. If you think about it, insects could take over the world; in a way, they have."

The castle hosted a celebration on the palace grounds for the humans and, of course, the dragonkind. The fairykind metamorphosed and became as large as humans; they couldn't remain that way for long, but it was fun for everyone to see them. The garden people brought veggies, fruit, nuts, and beans. The bakers brought sweet breads, pies, cakes, cookies, and all kinds of rolls. The liquid people brought all kinds of drinks. The music makers made much music. The white dragons made sky shows for everyone to see.

Marta and Yagoo asked Gorbash if he loved them, and Gorbash replied, "If I loved the originals, wouldn't I love the copies too?" They were happy with his answer, for you see, a copy does not feel itself to be a copy. They do not long for what they were; they are happy with what they are, copies or not. Gorbash said, "You cannot rush the future, nor can you hold it back. We tend to suffer consequences if we try to hold it back or even to rush it, as time has proved over and over."

Gorbash stood on a giant stage in front of the many ninety-foot reflection screens that were around the grounds, so that everyone could see it. He said: "Oh people of these wondrous lands and beyond, it is of the greatest importance that we learn to forgive our past and work toward a beautiful future. If we know the truth, we will come to learn it all. The fact is, we are a vital part of each other, an extension of each and every one of us. Welcoming love is the light within us all, the light that will shine a path for all weary travelers to walk in, and they in turn will be a springboard for others.

"As you go forth in life, take a look at others as you would yourself. Come to know and understand that you can learn to bring out the best in others as you pull out the very best in yourself. Try not to succumb to self-pity, lust, greed, and, most of all, judgmental hatred. There is no room for such things when life is filled to the brim with light and love. You see you are a bright beacon of hope for all those who are lost to the bleakness of the past. I do not speak of religion; I do not speak of politics; and I am not talking about what is found to be popular. I speak of what is truly right. We all know what is in our hearts, minds, and in our deepest consciences. A famous man once said those words—Martin Luther King Jr."

Is this book a true story?

Gorbash answers: I will answer that by saying this: all the lessons in this story are true if you choose to live by the beauty and wisdom of truth. But then, all the lessons in this story are false if you choose to live by the greed and vanity of falsehood.

Question: Were there really dragons?

Gorbash answers: Oh yes, and to this day, dragons exist—the dragons of the dragon realms. The rain forest is now the safe home (realm) for some of us dragons, but sometimes we wander off. Oh yes, we wander far-off. We are a good friend of the so-called Big Foot, and we protect them—wouldn't you? No! They do not stink. Is that surprising? We who live so much in the clean, cool cave waters would never stink. The yucca plant has a sweet, sudsy side to it that comes in handy for washing; you could use it too.

Chapter Twenty-One
Has Gorbash Met His Fighting Match Or More?

Did you really think that was the last of the dragon stories? Come on now! Read on . . .

There was a rumble, a shake, and a loud jarring sound. Yes, I know everything starts out this way, so this is no different—except for the largest gray dragon the world has ever seen. He stood on the stage in front of the huge screen for all to see. He proclaimed himself to be the dragon master, as he pounded his chest and roared out loud, "Who will dare to challenge me?" You could hear a pin drop if a pin would drop, which it didn't. This gray dragon stood twenty-five feet tall with a wingspan of twenty-five feet. His scales were gray stone with black mortar beneath them, and his feet were gray stone. This new dragon said, "Call me Stone, then when I fight you will want to call me Mountain. Come, all you dragons, fight me to the death, or give the kingdom to me now, for you can never ever win." At that very moment, Gorbash stood face-to-face with the king, while King Kohler stood on the balcony. The king asked Gorbash in a concerned voice, "Gorbash, tell me—are we all doomed?"

"Oh, my great King," Gorbash said as he shed tears. "I will never let this poor, sick dragon take over the kingdom to rule in death. Nor will I ever let the likes of him kill the dragons that came here on my word. But I will fight the intruding dragon, even if I have to die with him to stop him. Tell me, in your wisdom, if there is another way, where no one dies. Please tell me—I am lost."

The king leaned forward and told Gorbash, "Gorbash, you have the heart of a king, the greatest, most noble king that could ever be. Your heart is nobler than mine or anyone I've ever known. You have the answers inside of you; call on them. You will never again be lost for thoughts."

Gorbash said, "Thank you, my King; I knew you would help me." Gorbash quickly turned on a forty-five degree angle and flew up above the gray dragon intruder. But by that time, the gray dragon had beaten all the other dragons and was preparing to take off their heads with a flaming sword. Gorbash yelled, "Stone! Stop! It is I, Gorbash, whom you wish to fight. Leave the others alone, and let it be between you and me." Down Gorbash went, shaking the stage when he landed. It sounded like thunder, and a dark cloud of dust moved out from the floor.

The stone dragon said, "Gorbash, you're the eldest dragon of us all. You will be nothing to take down."

Gorbash pounded his chest and yelled, "Go ahead and try to take me down, Stone. You're the youngest pup of all dragons. You may be big, but your brain has been damaged by your ordeal, Stone. You can be helped.

"Shut up!" The stone dragon screamed as he shot flame back at Gorbash.

Gorbash put his hands together and smothered the flame. The stone dragon flew up high, pointing his feet at Gorbash, and moved at great speed. Gorbash grabbed his feet and slammed him down on the stage, causing the floor to crack. It knocked the wind out of the stone dragon and broke a wing.

Gorbash went to Stone's aid, telling the big dragon, "I am sorry; I didn't want to hurt you. I know you have experienced great hardship and sorrow from some of the knights here, just as I have, but those men have died a long time ago." Just at that moment Stone took a swing at Gorbash, but Gorbash was too fast for him. Gorbash grabbed his fist and told the stone dragon, "You don't want to strike me anymore than I want to break your arm, do you, Stone?" At that very moment Stone kicked Gorbash in the chest. Gorbash slid back from the blow. Gorbash said, "Stone, if you kick me again, I will be forced to break your foot. Do you really want a broken foot, Stone?" The big, young dragon brought both feet up and attempted to kick Gorbash again. Gorbash held onto both feet as he told Stone, "I can break both feet in a second, but I don't want to." Stone bit Gorbash in the arm and drew blood. Gorbash sadly broke one foot.

The young dragon started to cry like a baby. Gorbash held him in his arms and was crying too. Stone asked Gorbash, "What am I to do, Gorbash? I harbor such hate for the dirty rotten killers of my parents. Those human bastards tied me up as a child and made me watch the filthy good-for-nothings cut my family up. They left me tied to die as they rode away on their horses, laughing. A female dragon came and fed me. Oh Gorbash, she saved my life!"

Gorbash called for the female dragons from the healing center to come and heal Stone's wounds.

Pearl brought some food and drink and asked Stone, "Stone, do you remember me? I'm the one that fed you. I can never have a pup, because I gave my milk to save you. So I felt you were my pup. You have grown so much."

Stone started crying again, saying, "Yes, yes, I am your pup; it is so wonderful. I have a family now." Stone asked Pearl, "I have always loved you, and I wonder if you love me too."

Pearl cried as she hugged Stone, "Of course I love my pup; I thought of you for many years, wishing I could see you. I hoped you were well. But I found out you had problems," and tears filled her eyes.

Stone told Gorbash, "Gorbash, I have something to confess."

Gorbash told Stone, "No, no! No one ever needs confess anything. You don't need to tell us anything you don't want to."

"What I'm about to say," Stone said, "will make all the rotten knights want to kill me."

"You are in my protection," Gorbash told Stone. "No one will hurt you. You can call me a rotten knight too, if you like. I'm not really proud of being a knight, first of all, and last of all, I am a dragon."

Chapter Twenty-Two
The Story Is Told By Stone

Stone started telling his story as he was rubbing his bandaged foot, "I found the creepy knights that did that awful deed. They were trying to stab me in the neck, but they couldn't reach me. Only one knight, a good knight, wouldn't help them, and it looked like the other knights were getting ready to hang him. So I didn't harm him at all. I tied the others to trees while they laughed about what they did to me. I spat out flames and set the trees on fire. But I didn't enjoy it; it felt awful. I was angry that I didn't enjoy it. But, I never killed another knight.

"The good human knight thanked me for saving his life. He told me he was in my service. He dropped his sword on the ground, tore off his knighthood badge, and started to walk away. I asked him if he wanted a ride somewhere, and we traveled together for a year. The good knight met a human woman, and we said our good-byes. I have to admit now that I have missed him; I would like to see him again."

Gorbash told Stone, "we will find him, and you will see each other again. But remember, a friend is taken as a relative to us dragons, so you may have a lot of relatives to re-meet."

The king came to the stage with a paper decreeing that Stone's past actions against the knighthood were considered self-defense and that he should feel no guilt. And the queen wanted to make Stone a knight, but a good knight. Stone said "Yes, I think I could handle that, but please give me time to adjust to it all. On second thought, no! I don't think I want to be knighted, but thank you for the honor."

The king and queen had a big party for everyone in Stone's honor. Pearl brought a friend, a big, female stone dragon named Rocky. Stone and Rocky became mates, and they had a pup they named Clay.

Gorbash found the ex-human knight, his name was, believe it or not, Clay Hill, and he lived on castle lands with his wife and two children. It was a happy reunion. Clay Hill had named one of his children Stone. Neither Clay nor Stone ever became friendly with the human knights, but they both overcame their former hatred. There was too much love going around. Stone stood on the stage to tell everyone how happy he was. He thanked Gorbash for beating him. Stone said, "All the time, I only wanted someone to kill me." But he also said, "Thank you, Gorbash, for not killing me."

"Saving life is what we are all about," said Gorbash. "Thank you, Stone, for responding. You're a helper to the castle, and you always had it in you. Being of service is the best feeling one can have."

Just at that moment, Rythma received a transmission from another dragon. Her name was Healeon. Rythma went to Gorbash to tell him, but he already knew she was coming and would arrive in a day or two. Healeon wanted to know if the king and queen would let her stay for a while. She wanted to sign the treaty between dragons and humans. The king and queen said she was very much welcome to stay for as long as she wanted. Gorbash told Rythma to inform the king and queen of Healeon's problem so they wouldn't be shocked when she arrived. Gorbash told Rythma that Healeon was coming here to die. Rythma said, "Oh! I didn't know that, Gorbash."

Rythma asked for an audience with the king and queen. She told them that Healeon was a two-headed dragon. She had no wings and was only seven feet tall. She had no mate or pup and was coming to bid her dragon friends farewell. Healeon was a light tan color with long arms and legs and long fingers. For a dragon, she was fairly young and good-natured, with a kind heart. The queen came out to tell her people, via the big screen, about the new dragon's arrival. The queen told them everything about Healeon, and they were very excited about meeting her and having a welcome dinner in Healeon's honor. Everyone was busy readying for the occasion. Happiness filled the castle grounds. They were sad for Healeon's plight but happy to make her welcome. People even brought gifts they thought a lady dragon would like. Some people brought healing teas; others brought dried fish, sealing wax, silk ribbons, and colored metallic nail enamel.

When Healeon got to the castle gate, she was met by the lady dragons. Healeon was brought in by the assembly of the French monarch; she was very much loved and revered by the people of France. The assembly brought her up to the steps of the palace where the king and queen awaited her. Healeon was weak and had to rest for an hour, then she sat on a special chair to comfort her. The queen asked if she wanted to meet the people or to be alone. Healeon stated that she would love to meet people; she had thousands of gifts to hand out. The dragon head on the right was called Healie and the one on the left was called Leiony. Together they were Healeon. The two dragon heads shared one body, one heart, two arms, and two legs. Healie was more in charge, and Leiony was just off Healie's shoulders. Leiony was draining the life out of Healie, and therefore, they were both dying. The doctors said there was nothing that could be done; they were doomed.

Chapter Twenty-Three
The Dragon Surgery

The next day, when Healie and Leiony had a good night's sleep, Gorbash asked to talk to them alone. The queen had them meet in her royal room, where she usually met the press. Gorbash asked Leiony about her thoughts on the situation. Leiony said, "I want the doctors to put me to sleep so Healie can live; what is the sense of us both dying?"

Healie started crying, "No, no, that would be murder. If we both die, it's a shame, but if one is killed, it's murder."

Gorbash asked, "Tell me please, Leiony, what does life mean to you?"

Leiony answered quickly, "Well, it's my thoughts; that's all I am." Then she looked down at the floor, and spoke clearly, "If my thoughts die, I am dead, because I have no body to die."

Then Gorbash looked over at Healie and asked her, "What is it you love so much about Leiony?"

Healie said, "Well of course, it's her mind; she is wise and good and lets me know what she thinks." Then Healie said quickly, "My dear Leiony does not need a body to do that."

Gorbash put his head down as he spoke, "I may have a way to conserve both lives, so that no one has to die." Gorbash looked Leiony in the eyes as he said, "It will be somewhat like it is now," Gorbash put his fingers up to his forehead. "You will be one separate name, one separate body, but two separate thoughts." Gorbash put his hands together as he said, "You can be known as Healeon One and Healeon Two."

Leiony let out a squeal of delight, "Yes, yes I like it; let's go for it."

But Healie got up from her chair to walk away as she yelled, "No it's still murder, whatever way you say it. You're talking about cutting her head off. Well, I won't go for it."

Leiony spat down her chin as she said, "Guess what? I'm not your sister; I'm not even your half sister. I'm in the way, only a little head on your shoulders. If you won't okay this, I will cut my own head off." Leiony was crying so hard as she continued. "Gorbash's idea will allow us both to live. I want this so bad, Gorbash! Don't let her walk away until you can talk to her."

Healie sat on the chair next to Gorbash and asked, "How can this be done safely?"

Gorbash said, "I need a glass of water; we all need a glass of water." Gorbash drank a full glass of water and started talking. "I've been doing this surgery for fifty years, but only on humans. Gorbash took a breath and said, "I have done surgery on conjoined twins, people with large tumors, and more. I will need to extract certain parts of Leiony's brain from her head and place it next to Healie's brain. You will be two different dragons, and one will not know what the other one is thinking. Sometimes you both may want to talk at the same time but not very often. One can sleep while the other is awake; one of you can even move around while the other sleeps. I will tell you more when we are done. Time's wasting. Here's the trick: both heads have to be partly awake while it's being done. Now," Gorbash said, "ask me any other questions."

Leiony asked Gorbash, "Will I only be a thought? No one will know it's me, right?"

Gorbash struck back with, "You will introduce yourself as Healeon two. There will be no lies; you both will use the body in turns. Others will know who you are." Then Gorbash noted, "Healie will have to sign a paper to consent to this surgery, because you both will use the same body, but Healie will be the primary owner, and Leiony will be a tenant of sorts. I'm sure you both love each other enough to do this, right? You both will be better-off for this, much better than you are now. You will not be two-headed anymore."

Healie asked, "Gorbash, when should we do this?"

Gorbash replied, "Ladies, you will have to do this now. You may not live until morning. Take a look at yourselves—Healie is turning gray. She will die first, and then there will be no substance left for Leiony; she will just stop breathing. I will let you decide; you can find me in the next room." Gorbash left the room.

Leiony turned to Healie and asked, "Please can we live?"

Healie said, "Bring the doctor back in; we've no time to waste." Gorbash was already calling to set up the operation room with all the human doctors and nurses to assist in the surgery.

A medical team drove up to the queen's royal room with an emergency van. Three men got out and rushed the dragon inside the van then into the operation room. Everyone was scrubbed clean, and both dragons were brought into a soft twilight semi-sleep, but they remained awake. Rythma walked in with her scrubs on, ready to talk to the ladies and give them peace. Rythma said, "Please, don't worry your heads off. Sorry—I didn't mean to make a pun, but Gorbash has done this procedure many times, and he's never lost anyone. I will be here if you need to talk to me. This work would not be done except for the fact that you both are dying. It is a matter of an emergency." Then the door to the operating room closed and the hours ticked by. Gorbash worked with a team of doctors and nurses who have never done this surgery before. The dragons felt no pain; they had received an injection to prevent it. The doctors cut open both their skulls, their brains. Healie's brain was hardly touched; the doctors spliced parts of Leiony's brain next to it. Each brain worked independently of the other. Gorbash spoke to Healie and Leiony through the procedure. He mostly talked to Leiony in order to get the correct answers he needed to perfect the procedure. A team of doctors worked to remove Leiony's head and tie off some of the veins and arteries.

Leiony cried when they told her they were removing her head (she did not feel it), but she smiled when she realized that she hadn't lost consciousness. She softly said, "Thank you." The doctors reconnected a portion of the main arteries from the body to the new brain site.

Both dragons were awake and understood each step of the process. Gorbash worked on the brain surgery. It had to be perfect so that the different parts of the brains aligned perfectly. Nurses used a device to suck the excess blood away, keeping everything clean. Parts of the skulls were put together, and they used special glue to bond the outer skin layers that hold the skull snug. The skull was just a few meters larger than before. Gorbash placed a thin sheet of dragon skin between the two brains to prevent them from growing together. He inserted a drain tube to let excess blood drain away to avoid swelling. He would remove the tubes will be removed a few days after the surgery.

Thanks to evolution, humans have one hundred billion neurons in each three-pound brain; dragons have five hundred billion neurons in each eight-pound brain.

Of course, we knew something could go wrong, even though Gorbash had had previous success with this procedure. Something can always go wrong when the patient is so sick. Gorbash did everything he could to prevent any mishaps. The team was in the operating room for five hours, with no break and more to do. A human doctor came out of the operating room while Gorbash remained inside. The doctor told the others, "All we can do now is see if she is strong enough to recover, and it looks real good at this time." Then he added, "I sure wish we could have done this sooner; she's on her last limbs."

The night ran into day. It was one body but two dragons. Someone screamed; no one knew if it was Healeon One or Healeon Two. Gorbash asked, "Who speaks? One or two?"

The voice came back, "Who wants to know? My doctor or my nurse?"

Gorbash said, "Hello Healeon Two, this is your friend Gorbash. You're looking good."

Healeon two asked "How's one? Is she doing all right?"

Gorbash told her, "She's sleeping at the moment, but is there anything I can do for you?"

Two said, "I would like a looking glass if you don't mind."

When Gorbash brought her a mirror, she opened her eyes to take a look.

Two asked, "Am I beautiful?"

Gorbash replied, "Yes you are beautiful, but you always were beautiful." Gorbash checked her bandage and told her, "Try not to move your head, at least until morning."

Two laughed as she remarked, "Oh Doctor, where is my head?"

Gorbash leaned down and whispered in her ear, "My dear, this is your head." Just then the voice made a slight change; it was One.

"Gorbash," she said, "Is she all right?"

Gorbash smiled as he said, "Take a look in the mirror and ask her yourself." They could talk to each other by looking in the mirror. They could even tell who was who. They took turns thanking Gorbash for his fine work. Gorbash told them, "Thank the team; I couldn't have done it all by myself." Then Gorbash said, "Get some sleep now; your brains need darkness to rest; every brain needs to be in the dark to rest."

Healeon One woke up the next day, but Healeon Two was still asleep. The human doctors and nurses feared the worst; they thought Two was gone. Gorbash reassured them that if Two was still asleep; she needed it. Gorbash reminded the doctors and nurses that it was Two who had been first to wake after the surgery. Gorbash told them not to needlessly be upset. "Remember, everyone," he said. "Two is the strongest of them both." But the day moved into night, and Healeon Two was not awake. Gorbash had two dragon nurses at her side, so she could see them when she woke up. Gorbash had the doctors check her vital signs each hour, and he said she was doing well.

Early the next morning, she woke and said, *"Doesn't a lady get fed around here? I'm starving to death"* Everyone was laughing, clapping, and crowding around her bed. Gorbash told Healeon Two and the nurses, "*Only fluids right* now, *little lady.*"

Healeon Two said, "*Get* me a *mirror; I want* to *talk* to my *better half.*" A big beaming smile came over the mirror followed by tears.

Healeon One told Healeon Two, "*You have always been my better half.*"

Healeon Two told Healeon One, "*I have never been* as happy *and* well as I am now." And they kissed the mirror, twice, one kiss each.

Gorbash told Healeon, "Sorry to have to break up this happy meeting, but the French monarchs are to arrive in a week. I made a transmission to their ambassador to let them know how you were doing. So get well; the king and queen said we will have a big get-together when they arrive. For now, you need to take it easy." Gorbash added, "The doctors and nurses have prescribed lots of R and R for you both."

Gorbash
Male protector of life

Chapter Twenty-Four
Time Is Well Received

Time passed, and all was well a year after Healeon's surgery. Rythma was preparing to return to Koreg's school. She planned to take the treaty with her to show the other dragons at the school.

All the dragons were free, without the threat of being killed by the palace knights. The atmosphere in the kingdom was more relaxed; the dragons were not on guard as much as they had been before the treaty. The dragons were always ready to protect the children in their care. Healeon decided to go back with Rythma to the school, and they were happy with the decision. Healeon planned to be a vital part of the teaching and creative work at the center.

Rednor was doing well with his blood situation; he had given blood to Healeon during her surgery. Rednor took on a mate he met at the palace grounds; she is red also. She was about to birth a pup. Blacksma met a black velvet lady dragon; things were working out for them also. Seagon was giving many lectures on positive feelings and working to overcome his own hate of the knights. He told everyone that "Hate is a learned thing. So let us overcome and relearn a new way called love."

The Gypsy named Gypsy met a roving Wizard named, you guessed it, Wizard. They only wander around once a year for a month. It's hard to completely get the wandering out of you. Gypsy and Wizard were expecting to add a little wizard to their family very soon; their first. When they weren't wandering, Wizard and Gypsy lived at the castle and made healthy potions for the grounds.

Even later, Gorbash received a transmission from Healeon and Rythma. Healeon had mated with a French dragon she had known in France; he had loved them both. They all lived and worked at the teaching center.

Rythma mated with Isasor; they had always cared for each other. Koreg had no mate, because his focus was the children; he says that his focus will always lie with them.

The name Gorbash means be *good* for the *right* way, bringing smiles from the heart.

There within the castle lands, they all lived happily ever after: the people, the dragons, the animals, the children, and everyone therein.

Do You Know Where Your Dragon Is?

The lady dragon said to the male dragon, "Why are you tailing me?"

The little dragon said to the mama dragon, "Are these pajamas fireproof?"

Why were the little dragons standing on their heads at the dinner table?

Because mama dragon was serving pineapple upside down cake.

The sign on the door at the dragon motel read, "No smoking in bed."

Why do dragons have to pay in advance to stay at a dragon motel?

Because they don't want any fly-by-knights or dragonflies.

If you want a dragon for Christmas, just ask Santa Claws.

Have fun. Make up some dragon jokes and write them down on these blank pages.